WHAT DO YOU WANT FROM ME?

What Do You Want from Me?

AND FIFTEEN OTHER STORIES

Doris Dörrie

TRANSLATED FROM THE GERMAN BY

JOHN E. WOODS

ALFRED A. KNOPF

NEW YORK

1991

THIS IS A BORZOI BOOK
PUBLISHED BY ALFRED A. KNOPF, INC.

Copyright © 1991 by Alfred A. Knopf, Inc.
All rights reserved under International
and Pan-American Copyright Conventions.
Published in the United States by
Alfred A. Knopf, Inc., New York,
and simultaneously in Canada by
Random House of Canada Limited, Toronto.
Distributed by Random House, Inc., New York.
Originally published in Switzerland as
Was Wollen Sie Von Mir?
by Diogenes Verlag AG, Zurich
Copyright © 1989 by Diogenes Verlag AG

Library of Congress Cataloging-in-Publication Data
Dörrie, Doris, [date]
[Was wollen sie von mir? English]
What do you want from me? : and fifteen other stories /
Doris Dörrie ; translated from the German
by John E. Woods.
p.   cm.
Translation of: Was wollen sie von mir?
ISBN 0-679-40092-3
I. Title.
PT2664.O73W3713   1991
833'.914—dc20   90-45940
CIP

Manufactured in the United States of America
First American Edition

FOR MY HUSBAND

Contents

WHAT DO YOU WANT FROM ME?

Lies

SHE SAW HIM from the back first. Even seated, he was a giant who towered over all the other students. His head was too big, his neck too thin and long, his hair almost white. She nervously rubbed her hands together and tugged her skirt straight.

"Good morning," she said. "My name is Rosemarie Hüttner. I'm a photographer, and for the next hour I'd like to tell you something about portrait photography."

The students eyed her wearily. Several yawned in her face, one girl was knitting, only the giant looked at her expectantly, even gave her a smile. But it wrenched his face into a grimace, his mouth twitched, and one eye rolled about out of control. Everything about his face was wrong. It looked like patches sewn together—but not because of a bad accident, the whole head was too misshapen for that, the brow too high and wide. Like a hydrocephalic, Rosemarie thought, that might well be it. She tried not to stare at him, but he was sitting right in the middle of the room, with his white hair and his chalky pale skin.

She spoke about light.

"The first thing the eye always notices is the brightest spot on a photograph. You need to be aware of that before composing a picture."

The giant must have wandered in here by mistake, and she braced herself for him to start babbling wildly to himself. The students paid him as little attention as they did her. Their curiosity about their new teacher sputtered out within a few seconds. Only he seemed to listen attentively, hanging on her words with one eye, the other wandering askew.

Rosemarie pulled from her pocket a lightbulb on a cord.

"I'd like to try a little experiment with you," she announced with forced enthusiasm. "I'll need a volunteer to come up front here." Before she even finished her sentence, she knew what she was afraid of. And, sure enough, the giant rose clumsily to his feet and walked slowly toward her. The arms dangled like little appendages from his enormous body; he walked with knees slightly bent, carefully setting one foot in front of the other. "Maybe it'd be better," she said hastily, "if we started with a female face." What a stupid ploy, she thought. The giant stopped in his tracks, wrenched his face into another smile, slowly turned around, and went back to his seat. Then came a long pause. The students watched her for what would happen next. Rosemarie's armpits started itching. She pointed to a girl of average prettiness, who reluctantly stood up.

Rosemarie let down the blinds and switched on the lightbulb.

"You will now see how her expression changes depending on how I direct the source of light onto her face."

She wandered with her lightbulb around the girl's face, making it beautiful. The brow was a little too low—she made it disappear in darkness. She accentuated the classic straight nose, let a dimple cast a strong shadow.

"Photography has nothing to do with truth. The camera lies, and it's up to you how you let it lie. And you use light to do the lying." She held the lightbulb under the girl's chin, which made the face hard, bitter, and old.

"Never try to be objective. Objectivity is for the timid and half-hearted. Objectivity wants to be universal. The more subjective you are, however, the greater success you'll have in expressing something universal and valid."

She thanked the girl and was just about to turn

around and pull up the blinds, when the giant stood up again and moved resolutely toward her. She gesticulated helplessly with the lightbulb, but simply couldn't come up with a new excuse. In the semidarkness she saw her students shift expectantly in their seats. I can't, I simply can't, she thought. He calmly sat down in front of the class and looked eagerly at her. Then he nodded. Her heart was pounding as she tentatively raised the lightbulb and directed it onto his face—which promptly shattered into monstrous details, the gigantic brow looming white, the distance between the eyes so large now that one eye no longer seemed to have anything to do with the other. Terrified, she lowered the bulb. Use light to lie, use light to lie, she muttered to herself in a monotone.

She lifted the bulb high above his head to light it from the rear, and turned him into a madman with a halo. He went right on staring at her with the same imbecilic grin. She desperately tried to remember all her professional tricks for emphasizing a face's beauty and distinctive traits and allowing the rest to vanish in gracious darkness. But no matter where she looked in that face, she found nothing she could have used to make the rest forgettable—every inch of this mass of flesh betrayed the whole.

She covered the beam with her hand, let it skitter over his face, and succeeded only in creating one new monster after the other. Sweat streamed down her body. She had made fat politicians look distinguished, had turned old actresses young, had restored inspiration to drunken artists. Her light had lied with a vengeance, and now she couldn't persuade it to tell one tiny fib. The "Queen of Light and Shadow," a newspaper had once called her—but the fluorescent light in the bare room had dealt with him more kindly than she.

She stood there rigid, the lightbulb raised high in her hand. Turning toward her in surprise, he projected an oversized shadow on the wall, a profile so lacking in anything human it was like a great beast. She was shaking as she pulled the plug out of the wall socket. He said a soft "Thanks" into the darkness. She was considering making a dash for it, but then a student raised the blinds.

She couldn't recall later how she had got through that hour. Mute and disdainful, so it seemed to her, the students gathered up their books and notes and left the room.

She packed up her lightbulb and cursed it. He stood in the door, blocking her way. She looked up at him.

"May I ask you something?" he said in a soft, very gentle voice. She nodded, amazed that he could speak at all.

"If someone were to tell you that he would like to

become a photographer, but was terribly afraid of asking people if he could photograph them, what advice would you give him?" After a pause he added, "I presume you know who I'm talking about. Might I invite you to join me in a cup of coffee?"

He very carefully balanced the coffee on a tray as he moved ahead of her through the student dining hall, and Rosemarie sensed how the eyes of all the students were following their progress. She automatically took a chair on the side of the table that lay in shadows, and was immediately sorry she had. The giant sat down opposite her, and one of those lamps with a plastic orange shade, the kind you see in every coffeeshop, shone mercilessly in his face. He watched her, biding his time and stirring his coffee, slowly, ever so slowly. The spoon looked tiny in his gigantic hand. She did not look at him when she finally began to speak. "Everyone has fears," she said quickly. "And if I had no fears, I wouldn't take pictures. I started taking them to overcome my fear."

"What are you afraid of?" he asked amiably, laying his thick white hands on the table. All his movements were so deliberate they seemed to occur in slow motion.

"Oh, of . . . of the world. Especially of things I don't know. I photograph them so that I can get to know them and that way I don't have to be afraid of them anymore." Rosemarie could not recall ever having described her profession so clearly, even to herself.

"And? Does that work?" he asked gently.

"No," she said. And he began to laugh, and his whole face quivered and wobbled with delight. He snorted, tears of laughter zigzagging down his distorted face. Finally he managed to say, "So there's really no point in it?"

"No, not really. But while you're doing it, you always think it might work."

Still smiling, he took her hands in his. They were very warm and soft, like two big pillows. "You shouldn't be such a pessimist," he said and bent toward her. "Afraid of the world—well, if that's all." The lamp above the table shone on his ears. He had small, well-shaped ears, the prettiest ears she had ever seen.

The Sofa

IT WAS her habit to leave everything behind when she moved out—one plastic bag was enough. She left her men long before she moved out. The men were always very surprised, but couldn't explain why. Why now? Spock began to play chess while Linda tucked away her passport, toothbrush, and makeup, a few clothes, and her favorite pair of high heels. She had called him Spock from the start, because he had long pointy ears like Mr. Spock on "Star Trek."

"We had some real good times, right?" he said, and the only way Linda could tell that he felt anything was the way he held tight to the queen on his chessboard.

"Sometimes we had some real good times," she said.

The stuffy air in Furniture Paradise made her a little nauseated. Sullen couples shoved their way past her, some of them dragging fretting children behind them. They slumped wearily onto beds and sofas, studied catalogs—the men snapped measuring sticks open and closed, rocked doubtful heads; the women felt fabrics and tested for sturdiness; the children sat screaming on the floor or hopped around on beds until salesmen shooed them off. Linda could remember only one man it had been fun to shop with. But otherwise they hadn't been much of a match.

She steered toward a black sofa with red armrests, yellow pillows, and blue legs, sat down and watched Moses engross himself in a twenty-minute study of carpet patterns. She called him Moses because he was so wise. His wisdom had prevented him from getting into an argument with his wife about how to divide up the furniture. Linda had met her only once, after Moses suggested that the reasonable and adult thing to do would be to introduce his wife to his new lover. His wife had rubbed a table with furniture polish, Moses had talked about finances, and Linda had drunk a glass of orange juice. She hadn't liked their furniture. All gloomy antiques.

Moses came over and smiled.

"You're not serious about that sofa," he said.

"It looks Japanese," Linda said.

"Postmodern."

"I like Japanese food and I like this sofa."

He sat down next to her.

"It's uncomfortable."

He took Linda by the hand and stood up.

"But we won't argue about it."

"No," she said.

He chose a gray leather sofa. It matched his flannel pants. Linda thought it was cold and dull, but she didn't say so. She preferred to sit on the floor anyway. Like an Arab, Moses had observed. Which was why they were buying a sofa now. As she got up from the gray leather sofa, Linda noticed a sign on the armrest: SORRY, BUT I'M NOT AVAILABLE.

"What does that mean, not available?" Moses asked.

"They don't have it in stock."

Whenever he got angry he would break into smiles.

"The Japanese one is."

"Linda, darling, the Japanese one may be available, but it is not available to us."

"Why?"

"Because—beg your pardon—I think it's tasteless, and one shouldn't argue about taste."

He always said "beg your pardon" whenever he would permit no contradiction. Spock had been the first to notice this, not her. They had played chess together for years, without ever having become friends. Spock was forever saying, "If he tells me 'beg your pardon, but that wasn't a good move,' one more time, I'll kill him." But he usually lost to Moses.

Spock's lack of manners had got on her nerves, and Moses' politeness was starting to get on her nerves today, in this damn Furniture Paradise.

Moses went looking for the nearest saleswoman to ask if the gray leather sofa was really not available. He loved boring discussions. Linda didn't like even to ask people for directions. She would rather wander around lost than hear some long explanation she wouldn't remember anyway.

Moses would never leave his hotel in an unfamiliar city without a map, she was sure of that, and suddenly she lost all desire ever to take a trip with him.

She had always got along with Spock best when they were traveling. They had gone halfway around the world with almost no luggage, no plan, no goal. They had sat around in some airport or other for days on end because they didn't want to bother with inquiring ahead of time about flights. Their trips consisted for the most part of being stranded somewhere, waiting for their trip to continue.

There is a picture for every love affair. Spock and Linda at some godforsaken bus stop in the jungle, waiting, he with his travel chess on his knees, she with her head on his shoulder. That is about how the picture of their five-year love affair would look. She would hang it on the wall above the Japanese sofa.

Linda sauntered slowly into the kitchen department and left Moses with his saleswoman, who was melting visibly under his charms and would do everything possible.

Spock was no different on a trip than he was at home. It had taken a long time for her to understand that. He waited. He spent his whole life waiting. At home he waited for emotions that Linda had delivered up gladly and lavishly at the start, on trips he waited for buses and planes. That was the only difference.

Moses hated to wait. He tried as much as possible to prevent getting into situations where he would be forced to wait. Linda needed only to lean back and wait for what Moses planned for her, day in and day out. Buying furniture, for example. It was pleasant to have someone else organize your life. Linda could understand Spock now.

As she came strolling back to the sofas from the kitchen department, Moses and the saleswoman had disappeared. She decided to sit down on the Japanese sofa and wait.

There sat Spock. His hair was shorter. His pants were cleaner.

He didn't see her until she was standing right in front of him. She sat down beside him.

"You like this sofa?" Spock asked.

"Yes," she said, "it's tasteless."

"Beg your pardon," he said.

They both smiled. A little.

"How are you doing?" she asked.

"She doesn't like our furniture."

"She doesn't like our furniture?"

"No," he said. "She thinks it's tasteless."

"She's right about that," Linda said.

"That's why we liked it so well."

"Why I liked it. I bought it, not you."

"That's true," he said. "You can have somebody come get it if you want. She'll throw it out otherwise."

"I don't want it," Linda said.

"Beg your pardon," Spock said.

"Idiot." She laid her hand on his knee.

"And now what?" he asked.

"Nothing." She took her hand away again.

"You going to buy this sofa?"

"Maybe."

"Maybe I want to buy it, too."

They looked at each other and said nothing.

"What do you think, Linda? When's the next bus?"

"Tomorrow. Day after."

"Mañana."

"Stop it, Spock."

They both stood up at once, and without looking at each other again went off in different directions.

Moses was coming toward Linda. He was waving a piece of paper. "Got it," he said, "it'll be delivered tomorrow morning. It's the last one and we got a discount because it was on display."

He gave Linda a kiss and pulled her toward the exit.

When she turned around she saw Spock and a slender, blonde woman sitting on the gray leather sofa. Two salesmen were talking with them; they stood up. One salesman pointed to the sign: SORRY, BUT I'M NOT AVAILABLE. Then they carried off the sofa.

The blonde woman turned angrily to Spock. He shrugged and pointed at the Japanese sofa. The woman gave a decisive shake of her head, took Spock by the arm, and pulled him away. As he turned for one last look at the Japanese sofa, his eye caught Linda's.

Moses took Linda by the hand.

What Do You Do While I'm Gone?

I ASK HIM: "What do you do while I'm gone?"

"Nothing," he replies, "nothing at all. I warm up some food and then make myself comfortable in front of the television." I can't believe that. Just sits down in front of the TV and eats his supper. It happens about once or twice a month. It's got so I can tell when he needs another evening to himself. That's what he calls it, and he can't even look me in the eye, but just says very softly, "Honey, I think I need an evening to myself."

Maybe he always did it, even before we met. Maybe I simply didn't notice. He was so normal, a little boring maybe, but he was good to me; he brings me my coffee in bed even now. If his buddies at work only knew. But no one knows except me, just me. And I'm proud of that. We have a real secret. We'd been married for over two years before he told me. And suddenly I didn't think he was boring anymore, not at all. It isn't normal, and what isn't normal can't be boring. I used to ask if I couldn't just stay home and watch him, but he only got mad, why should I begrudge him just one evening to himself every other week? All I wanted was to watch him, just sit on the couch and watch him. What could be so awful about that? I don't believe he just sits there, watching TV and eating. I've been walking around now for two hours, and he needs at least four. I'm not allowed to come home early, that's part of our agreement.

When we first met he loved to give me presents, lingerie or maybe a lipstick. He could spend hours at a department-store cosmetic counter picking out the right-color lipstick, almost drove the saleswomen crazy, but he wouldn't give up till he had found the right color, and sometimes I thought, why is that so important to him really? What man attaches that much importance to the color of a lipstick? But I didn't notice a thing, not one thing.

Yes, I was flattered that he liked to watch me dress, or, even more, get undressed, but every man likes that after all. He bought me all my lingerie; he didn't like it when I wore my cheap cotton panties. And it had to be black, or red. And silk. Always silk. He put out a fortune for it. That does feel good, silk against your skin, but there are more important things, it seems to me. But it was important to him. And I love him.

Despite everything, I do love him, otherwise I would never have agreed to this. Back when it started I went to the movies or visited girlfriends, but over the years that's got less and less interesting. I'd like to know what he does while I'm gone.

He told me about it while we were sitting together watching TV—it was a quiz show—said it was all perfectly normal. But sometimes he just felt this need and couldn't do anything about it. He had tried everything to suppress it, but there'd be something missing if he couldn't do it, and so this was better really than him coming to hate me someday because he couldn't do it. I laughed and was a little confused, but I didn't think all that much about it, not at the start. I wanted him to be happy.

He uses my things. We're about the same size. So he didn't spend all that money on me. Or not just on me. I've asked myself whether he still loves me. But otherwise everything is perfectly normal. Not as passionate as it was once, maybe, but we have a better marriage than most people. I know that from talking with my girlfriends. I haven't breathed a word of it to them. It's our secret. Does he use the black or the red? What does he do for shoes? Mine wouldn't fit him at all. I don't ask him, I know that he doesn't like that. My blue dress, he likes that one so much. On me. Or maybe no dress at all? He has a good figure: His hips are smaller than mine; he's slender, very slender, although he eats more than I do. I just have to look at a piece of chocolate and my hips show it. I have to count every calorie; he laughs at me. I wonder how he'd like it if all of a sudden I had to wear clothes three sizes larger—he'd have to go out and buy his own clothes.

Maybe he would stop then, who knows? It's not that I really want him to stop. I want him to be happy. Here I am going around this block for the fourth time. When I get home I ask him sometimes what was on TV. He always knows, every detail. But he can't just sit there, can he? Wonder if he puts on makeup? He has such a beautiful mouth, big, but not too big. My lips are thin in comparison.

I just can't picture him like that. I can picture him doing everything else, though, I've known him for so long now. I know how he sits in his office and stares out the window, what he looks like when he's brushing his teeth, standing there naked in the bathroom, what he looks like asleep, or when he cleans his fingernails with a matchstick. I don't like that much. He has very short fingernails, cuts them every week. Wonder if he uses nail polish? And then removes it before I get home? Goes to all that trouble just to sit in front of the TV? I used to get dressed up a lot myself. For him. Or when we went out someplace.

But all by yourself? Why bother? He does it to please himself, he says, nobody else. And it has nothing to do with me.

Our apartment is right over there, ground floor. From the front yard you can see right into the living room. The curtains are heavy and thick, he insisted on that, I'd rather have none at all. The day we moved in he said there had to be curtains at the windows. Maybe because he already knew what he wanted to do. We've hardly changed over the years. I have more wrinkles, more than he has, his skin is thick, a man's skin, it doesn't crease so easy. I look older than he does already. And I'm two years younger, and always will be. Everything will always be like this. I'll go for a walk, for hours, every two weeks, sit in a bar in winter and have a few brandies . . . it'd be so much easier for me if I only knew what he does. Then there'd be some point. It's not that I want him to stop. I really do want him to be happy.

I know I shouldn't. But it's so easy to climb over the low hedge, and the curtain isn't quite closed, I mean, just one quick look.

My heart is pounding, suddenly I have the idiotic feeling I'm cheating on my husband, right at this moment. I close my eyes, I see him in his suit, just like every morning when he goes to work, a real man. Then I peep through the little slit in the curtains. I pulled them back before I left, just the least bit; he didn't notice.

I can see our living room, the blue light from the TV reflected on the wall behind the couch. I just stare at the wall, then very slowly move my eyes down, over the painting with the winter landscape, to the brown armrests of our leather couch. I can see my black bra, the lace one, my stockings with the little silver dots up the sides, my red shoes, heels sticking way out, and then I see her, a woman, a very beautiful woman. She has a tray on her knees, she's eating slowly and meticulously, never looking away from the TV, a woman, with red lips, beautiful, large lips, her legs crossed slightly, long, slender legs. She sits there calmly, smiling at something on TV. She looks happy. And beautiful. More beautiful than me.

Are You a Witch?

I'M NOT ASLEEP, but the others think I'm asleep. I can hear Herbert laughing in the next room; the kids are screaming. Sweet sleep is on the run; I can't hold on to it any longer. I hear them giggle. My heart starts pounding. There's nothing I can do about it. I try to calm myself. It pounds harder. I don't know why. Thudding in my ears—my heart.

"Ninety-nine, a hundred, ready or not here I come," Juliane shouts in the next room. Herbert laughs. He never laughs like that with me. Never. He picks the kids up at his wife's place on Friday afternoon. Every Friday afternoon my heart starts to pound.

Babette has just turned three. "My mommy says you're a witch," she tells me. "Are you a witch?"

I'm twenty-three. I fell in love with Herbert on vacation. His wife and two kids were with him. I knew all about it. He looked lonely on the beach. We met by chance the first time, both out for a long, lonely walk on the beach, then we met every day behind a big rock. His wife is ten years older than he. She looks hard. I didn't like her. She reminded me of my Latin teacher. She made his life difficult, he told me. We didn't talk all that much, behind the rock.

I was twenty-two, I didn't know what to say to a thirty-four-year-old man with a family. He knew how to build a fire. That was more than most men I knew. I'd bring a couple of potatoes along, a piece of meat, sometimes a fish. He built the fire. He knew how to fish, too, he said. He looked like he did, too. Like someone who would take care of you.

No one ever saw us behind our rock.

As they were driving away, our cars met on the narrow road to the village. We drove very slowly past each other. He was at the wheel. I was alone in my car. He nodded to me. The kids were crying in the back seat. I nodded back. His wife gave them some candy.

I went back to the rock alone once. I found his footprints and put my feet in them.

When I saw him again in a department store in Munich, our tans had already faded. Babette was holding on to his hand. She wanted a black doll. She screamed. He bought it for her. He said softly to me: "I moved out four weeks ago." Babette swung her black doll and watched me.

• • •

He had moved into the apartment of a friend who had gone to India for a year.

After that first night I spent with him there, I just stayed on. I called my roommates and said I wouldn't be coming back. They could do what they wanted with my stuff.

I asked him if he loved me. And he always answered: "You wouldn't be here otherwise."

We were alone for three months, behind the rock. Then he and his wife came to an agreement about visiting rights.

"My mommy says you're a witch," Babette tells me.

When the kids were here, he wouldn't look at me.

I went to the movies a lot on weekends. When I got home the kids were in bed. He would be lying between them. "You're an adult," he told me, "they aren't."

The kids didn't like my spaghetti sauce. They looked at me and didn't say a word, and didn't eat. Herbert took their plates and dumped the spaghetti in the garbage. He cooked them the kind of sauce they were used to.

In the little room where I sleep, I wake up the minute they hit the floor. They are quiet, they've been taught well. But I wake up all the same. My heart starts to pound. I keep my eyes closed for as long as I can. Then I hear him romping with them and laughing. Sometimes I can fall back to sleep again when they're all in the bathroom together. But at some point I have to get up, because otherwise my pounding heart will smother me. I've tried coming out of my room with a smile. He doesn't look at me. I've tried joking with the kids. He doesn't look at me. Monday, I think, it'll be Monday soon, then he'll look at me again.

"Nothing is more certain than doubt" is what he often says. I don't understand what he means.

"Do you love me?"

"You wouldn't be here otherwise."

I have to get up. My heart is pounding in my stomach, in my ears, in my head. Babette screeches with glee. Herbert is rumbling like an airplane.

I open the door. He is playing pilot with Babette.

"Where's Juliane?" I ask.

"Oh, she's playing hide-and-seek," Babette says as she flies through the air on his hands.

I look at my swollen face in the bathroom mirror. It always looks like this on weekends. When I turn off the water I hear whimpering coming from the hallway closet. Juliane is crouching behind the clothes.

She uses the hem of my red dress to wipe her nose. She refuses to come out. I sit down beside her in the closet. She is crying. I don't say a word.

"Close the door," she whispers. We can hear Babette and Herbert laughing in the distance.

"Why are you in the closet?" She doesn't answer, pulls my dress over her head. So we just sit there; she sniffs now and then. No one is looking for us.

Suddenly, very suddenly, as if I had turned back to some page in my brain, I remember. "You were playing hide-and-seek, weren't you?"

She nods. "And you found this great place to hide. You closed the door, Babette yelled, 'Here I come.' Was she going to find you? And your heart started to pound a little." Juliane pulls my dress away from her head and looks at me. Even in the dark I can see her damp eyes glistening. "And you heard her looking for you, but she didn't find you. Your hiding place was so good she couldn't even find you." She nods. "Did Babette call your name?"

"Once."

"Only once?"

"Once daddy, and once Babette."

"But you didn't want to give away where you were, so you just didn't come out. And then all of a sudden they didn't call your name anymore. Then everything got very quiet. No one was looking for you now. The game was over. And now you're not sure how you're supposed to get out of the closet. Right?"

We can hear Babette's squeals and Herbert's laughter.

"My heart is pounding so funny," Juliane says.

The Mermaid

FOR HOURS NOW Ella had been lying motionless on her bed. Above her hovered the little mermaid made of green wood. As always, she was looking in her mirror and combing her hair with her delicately carved comb.

"Did I do something wrong, Anton?" she had asked him. From the way he had turned his back to her and smoothed his jeans, Ella knew he was about to cut out. He closed the bathroom door gently. That was another sure sign.

She let an egg slide into the little red pot, the one with the dent, and watched the beads of air rise to the surface. Three weeks ago they had brought in a woman who drowned and left her body to science in her farewell note. "I wouldn't do it," Ella thought. "I wouldn't want students cracking jokes about me." She set the timer for four and a half minutes.

She had already known two weeks ago, when Anton hurled the little red pot against the kitchen wall and screamed: "I don't know! I don't know anything! I don't know what you want from me, and I don't know what I want from me!"

She put the egg in a green egg cup and a slice of toast on the plate, poured some orange juice into a glass, and carried it all back to her bedroom. She could hear him showering.

She took his books from the nightstand and laid them outside the apartment. Two pairs of red underwear he kept at her place, his sunglasses, including the lens that had fallen out, the thick socks she had lent him when the heat was off one weekend last March. They had stayed in bed for two days, and Ella had thought she was happy.

Anton came out of the bathroom. "I'm sorry," he said. Ella nodded and cracked open her egg.

"It's not your fault."

"Yours either," Ella said.

"Maybe we could . . ."

"Be friends?"

"Yes," he said.

"Maybe," Ella said. The egg was a little too soft. He banged his fist on the doorframe, then pulled a pack of cigarettes from his pants pocket.

"Want one?" He held the pack out to her. She had

bought them last night in the Chinese restaurant on the corner. He hadn't said a word, just drummed on the table with his chopsticks. I knew then already, too, she thought.

He gave her a light. Now he's wondering if he ought to give me a kiss, Ella thought. Anton shrugged and tried a shaky smile. She looked at his sneakers. The soles were ripped at the toe, and as he left the room they flapped open and shut like two mouths.

"The key!" she called after him. Then she heard him fumbling with his key ring, a soft "ping" when he laid the key on the glass table beside the door.

He pulled the door shut energetically behind him. The mermaid rocked gently in the draft.

The Indonesian woman who had sold Ella the mermaid had had a beautiful face and told her how on Bali they hang these wooden figurines above the cradles of newborn babies to watch over the first year of life. The mermaid Ella picked out was the only one that had wings as well as a fish's tail; she smiled into her mirror and combed her long wavy carved hair. Ella would have liked to ask the Indonesian woman if the mermaid had already watched over a baby and used up her powers as a guardian angel, if she could watch over adults, too, European adults. She didn't ask so that she wouldn't be disappointed. The Indonesian woman carefully removed the mermaid's arms, wings, comb, and mirror and packed each piece in printed tissue paper.

Ella carried it home as carefully as if it were a raw egg and had the feeling the mermaid kept her from getting hit when she crossed the street against the light.

In the little grocery next door she bought a bottle of Piccolo. She lit a candle, reassembled the mermaid, sprinkled it with the champagne—and turned it into the personal guardian angel of Ella Koch, age thirty-two, single, assistant professor of pathology.

When she went to hang the mermaid over her bed, one of the wings fell off. She stuck it back on with some airplane glue and drank the rest of the Piccolo.

Three days later she met Anton in the supermarket. He was three pfennigs short at the checkout, and the fat checkout girl with the bad black dye-job insisted he pay up. If she had been younger, Anton's charm and good looks would probably have melted her. Ella helped him out. Two weeks later he deposited both pairs of red underwear in her dresser.

She laid her breakfast to one side, turned over on her stomach, and closed her eyes. The noise from the street drifted into the room like a heavy curtain woven of honks, wailing motors, screeching trams, and the gentle whine of motorcycles as they took the corner.

It's summer, Ella thought, the motorcycles are whining. The whole world is busy. I should call the institute. She was glad that today she wouldn't have to see any students who cracked dumb jokes to cover up their horror, held their noses because they couldn't stand the odor, turned pale. The more nauseated they felt, the more asinine the remarks.

Ella did not understand why the individual components of a human being so terrified her young students; she had always admired the perfection of each part, and feared the living whole.

She opened her eyes and saw one of Anton's black hairs on her pillow. Should she save it, she wondered. She turned on her back and gave the mermaid a little push with her foot.

She's my witness, she thought, she saw it all. She knows the trouble I went to. But it was easy with him. At the start. When he was still a stranger. I was so in love with him.

And then one day she noticed his gigantic adam's apple, how it bobbed up and down when he spoke. She couldn't stop watching it: Before her very eyes Anton fell apart, became his components. He told her about his father, who had been a doctor, and that that was why he had been unable to study medicine. Ella watched his adam's apple and knew the dangerous spell had been broken, he would never break her heart. She had fallen out of love and so tried all the harder to love him.

The telephone rang thirteen times before it fell silent. Had he forgotten something? Of course he let it ring exactly thirteen times, that was him all over—stupid details. His fat little feet, his thick pelt of chest hair, his long nose that he always bored so deep into the pillow that it bent to one side and deformed his face—folded gristle. Ella wanted to remember the whole Anton, but had no luck. The individual parts kept forming new patterns, like in a kaleidoscope. She could no longer find her Anton, her handsome Anton.

The indifferent mermaid went on combing her hair. Ella laid her on the soft, bouncy mattress and tore off her wings and arms. Bereft of her mirror, her pretty painted face gazed listlessly now into the distance. Ella spat in the mermaid's face. "You didn't watch over me!" she shouted angrily.

Ella felt ridiculous, got dressed, and left the house. The woman ahead of her in the bus had yellow hair, sprayed stiff. She would have liked to touch it.

She prowled department stores, perfumeries, and boutiques, she was prepared for a long, long search for one certain color, one certain scent, one certain detail, for the magic formula that would restore her equilibrium. But the objects all pulled back from her. She felt a silk blouse for a few seconds too long, she walked up and down the counters once too often, she sprayed herself with too many perfumes, tried out too many different lipsticks on her wrist. Behind her back the saleswomen wrinkled their noses and shuffled their feet impatiently. They have a third eye for people who don't know who they are and where they're going.

The back of Ella's neck registered their disparaging looks; beads of sweat collected along her collar and ran down the front of her blouse like a strand of pearls. Please, she wanted to shout, tell me how it's done, how you float above the earth like that. "You can't go wrong with this body powder with gold dust," one saleswoman claimed, and Ella bought it for the box, a pink heart-shaped box. Hearts that no longer beat—she had often held them in her hand, red lumps, but clearly constructed, no curlicues, and definitely no romantic bowers for lovers and their candor.

Along with the body powder with gold dust, she bought some lace-trimmed silk panties, and added a lipstick with the very promising name Mon Rouge. Just one more ingredient was missing for her magic formula, and now she chose a perfume, sure it was the right one, a man's cologne that smelled vaguely of sweat.

In front of the perfumery, a young man sat holding

a sign: I AM HUNGRY. She gave him two marks. That put the final touch on her ritual, so to speak.

On the way home she began to run. The objects she had assembled with such care bounced in the plastic bag, she had to use them quickly, she knew how fleeting their effect could be—within a hour, by morning at the latest, they would no longer combine into a formula, would be useless junk. She flung the door closed behind her and at once slipped into her silk panties, painted her lips with Mon Rouge, dabbed her wrists and earlobes with perfume, dusted her body with powder. In her haste she dropped the heart-shaped box; it broke.

The light in her bedroom had turned blue now; the noise from the street had ebbed away. Ella gave the mermaid back her wings, her arms, comb, and mirror. Then she lay down on her bed. Her white panties shone in the darkened room, her lips tasted chic, the powder glistened golden on her body, she was fragrant with elegance and the great, wide world.

The mermaid hovered above her, looking in her mirror and combing her hair.

I'm Sorry

MY MOTHER likes him, my Calvin from Brooklyn. She changed her dress for supper and flirts with him as she passes the plate of cold cuts. She speaks only a few words of English, so she talks to Calvin in German and then pauses like a politician so that I can translate. "You can only get this kind here, and only at Wolf's butcher shop. It's called town sausage. Stadtwurst. Do you like it? Help yourself. You can manage a little more. You're as skinny as a rail." Pause. In English I tell Calvin he's supposed to eat another slice, otherwise she'll be offended again. My mother looks at me suspiciously. "He doesn't talk much, does he?" she says. "Just like your father. Have you told him about your father?" "Why not?" I say. "That's typical," she says, and silently reproaches me with her eyes.

My father left her six years ago, for a druggist who

had sold him the same Christmas and birthday present he got for my mother year after year, a perfume called Joy. For six years now my mother has claimed she always loved him more than he loved her. When I was still fairly young she told me a woman always ought to find a man who loves her a little more than she loves him, adding that meaningful smile of hers that could only mean "just like me." I felt sorry for my father.

My mother stands up and clears the table. A whiff of Joy drifts through the room. Calvin and I throw each other kisses behind her back. He loves me, I know that. He is sitting at the head of the table under the painting of a gloomy winter forest, just as my father used to. He is living in Cologne now with Brigitte the druggist. When I called from New York he said, "Don't tell your mother I'm happy."

She comes back from the kitchen with a bowl of raspberry pudding. I can tell she's powdered her nose again.

"Rote Grütze. Rote Grütze," she says very slowly to Calvin and smiles at him. "I'd love to go for a breath of fresh air," he says to me. "Later," I reply. "What did he say?" my mother asks. "He likes your raspberry pudding." I sound like her when I speak German. "It's wonderful to have you here again," my mother says. "I'll never understand why you're so determined to study over there. The filth in New York must be simply incredible. And so many people!" "I like the filth," I say. "Tell your mother how clean Germany looks to me," Calvin says at the same moment. I don't have to translate. My mother beams at him.

Calvin's last name is Weintraub. He was the first Jew I ever met and the first man whom I think I really love.

It was his suggestion to come to Germany during summer vacation. "You're probably more afraid than I am," he said to me, and he took my hand as our Lufthansa flight took off for Munich from New York. I flinched when the pilot came on and snarled in pure Prussian commando: "Zis is Captain Müller und his crrrew. Ve velcome you on boart und vish you a heppy flight." Calvin laughed. I'm the one who is suddenly afraid at German passport control, not him. All of a sudden I saw an old Nazi in every German over sixty-five—didn't he?

"He's good-looking," my mother says. I translate this for Calvin. "Tell her that you get your beauty from her." I tell her this and she turns red, giggles like a little girl, and suddenly looks very young. I would love to have inherited her reddish blond hair. I have my father's brown eyes and almost black hair. People in America never took me for a German, which I found flattering.

My mother claps her hands. "Now I've got a surprise for you." She proudly places a bottle of sparkling wine on the table. Calvin and I exchange grins. Under the table he lays a hand on my knee. We're both thinking of all the bottles of Moët we've shared on the Brooklyn Bridge by the full moon. Where I told him that my mother is fifty-four and my father fifty-six; just casually mentioned it, and let him do the arithmetic. "You trying to make me feel uncomfortable, or yourself?" he asked.

My mother turns on the radio. Bavarian marches. Calvin's polite smile freezes on his lips. But only I notice. My mother raises her glass. I stand up and turn off the radio. Calvin gives a slight shake of his head.

"You're right," my mother says, "it's a lot cozier without the tootling." Did she understand? Did she understand any of it? We toast. "Calvin Weintraub," she says, "what a lovely name."

I insisted that Calvin and I both sleep in my old room, my teen-age room. My mother wanted us to have the marital bed she has slept in alone for six years now. She still makes up both sides, every three weeks. "It'll be so uncomfortable for you two in that old bed," she says and I know how difficult it is for her to say it. I'm the one who blushes.

She has put my old teddy bear on my bed. It's missing one ear. The brand name is stuck in the other one, a button. Teddy bears are as German as the Black Forest and German shepherds.

"I'm sorry, Calvin," I say. "What are you sorry about?" he asks, and I can feel his breath on the back of my neck; we both fit on my narrow old bed only if we lie on our sides. "I'm sorry it's all as real as it is." "Don't make it worse than it is." "It's worse than I thought." "No," he says, "it is what it is." His kisses make a pattern on my back; he holds my breasts in both hands. "We have to be very quiet," I say and cuddle against him.

She is wearing a folksy dirndl and sitting at the breakfast table, waiting for us. The coffee is cold. I cannot recall her ever wearing a dirndl before. Why today of all days? Why for Calvin of all people?

She has boiled some eggs and made sandwiches for our excursion. "We can always eat lunch in a restaurant somewhere," I say.

"You have no idea how expensive everything is now." "More expensive than New York?" I ask and I sound more snappy than I intended. She always has to talk about money. "I get seven hundred marks a month from your father. Seven hundred total." "Pardon me," I say, "I didn't mean it that way." "No," she says pointedly, "of course you didn't mean it that way. You've always taken your father's side."

She pours Calvin his coffee, smiles at him. She stops smiling to say, "Have you talked with your father? Of course you have." "If you already know, why do you ask?" "Did he tell you how happy he is with her?" "No," I say, "we didn't talk about that at all." She is silent and smiles—smiles. "No point in going on our little trip now, it's already eleven," she says. I would like to paste those hard-boiled eggs onto her smile. "What about our trip?" Calvin asks.

We drive by way of Hof to the border of the GDR. The idea could well have been hers. But Calvin wants to see it, because he can't imagine it. "HALT! FOR AMERICAN PERSONNEL. 50 M. TO BORDER," the sign announces. Calvin is impressed. My mother says nothing. She knows I can't stand how she goes on about the Russians. "The Russians are so close here," Calvin says, "you can't even imagine it in America." "What did he say?" my mother asks. "That he's hungry," I say.

You can hear her suck in air. "That's the Todesstreifen there," she says to Calvin. "Death zone," I translate. "Is it really called that?" he asks. No one believes anything I say.

We drive through fields, the grain glistening white in the sun. It's the smell of summer vacation, of swimming pools and Nogger ice cream. "God, it's beautiful," Calvin says. Yes, it's beautiful, a beautiful country. He turns on the car radio. American Forces Network is giving the baseball scores. Calvin laughs. "Are you going to marry him?" my mother asks and plows ahead without a pause: "Excuse me, I forgot, it's not the sort of question I'm allowed to ask. How long are you going to stay on in America? May I ask that?" "You can ask anything you want," I say, and for the moment I mean it. "Maybe, maybe we'll even get married. But don't tell him I told you so." My mother turns around to me and winks. "How can I? I don't even know what the word is in English. It's 'marry,' isn't it?" "She just asked whether we're going to get married, right?" Calvin says. "No," I say, "she only asked what the English word is." "That's the same thing, isn't it?" he says and turns the radio up.

We drive along the Czech border. "After the '68 invasion my father bought himself a pistol," I tell Calvin. "But one day he got drunk and tried it out at the local shooting club; it wouldn't fire." My mother laughs. "You telling him about that stupid pistol? That was typical. Typical of your father."

She turns down a side road, and I don't notice where we're headed, until it's too late. A large sign reads: FLOSSENBURG—2 KM.

I went there once with my school class, to Flossenburg Concentration Camp Memorial. One girl cried. She had been left back a year and was older than we were. She was the only one who had any conception. I remember we put itching powder down a boy's back on the way home. That's when I cried.

Damn my empty-headed mother, who thinks Weintraub is a lovely name. If I tell her she should turn around, she'll ask me why. And I'll have to explain. How am I going to explain? Wonder if Calvin recognized the name? He is leaning forward now, concentrating on baseball scores.

WELCOME TO FLOSSENBURG, YOUR HOLIDAY TOWN, on a banner spanned clear across the street. Tourists in red knee stockings and knickers tromping through town. A very small sign points the way to the Concentration Camp Memorial.

A fat child dashes across the road. My mother honks. Calvin looks up. I feel sick. "Yippie!" he shouts. The Mets won. We leave Flossenburg behind. I want to go back to America.

My mother has detailed dinner plans. "I want to show Calvin the town," I say. "But I've already defrosted the roast," she says. "You no sooner get home and off you go again." As we depart she is watching TV in her dirndl. "It's not your fault," I want to tell her, because she looks so sad, but what I'm thinking is: "It's all your fault."

I drag Calvin to a fast-food joint and disco near the American barracks. Black GIs, kids really, are hanging out on the street, giggling German girls stroll up and down in front of them and wiggle their behinds. The GIs shout obscenities after them. "Why did you bring me here? So I can be embarrassed by the American army?" Calvin asks. No, because I feel safe from Germans here. But I don't tell him that. I say, "I only wanted to show you where it was I started to dream of America, here in these discos; they were playing 'Ship of Fools' and I was fifteen." They are almost all still here: Metropol, Stardust, Moonlight, and Eden. I show him my regular spot in the far back corner with a view to the dance floor. I was a wallflower, almost never danced, just watched. Calvin is touched. Behind us two girls are necking with two GIs. They tell each other in German what they think of their conquests. "Mine kisses real wet, really slobbers," one tells the other. They are almost convulsed with laughter. The two blacks share uncomprehending grins and watch them. They are drinking pale ale. I picture them sauntering along the boardwalk at Coney Island, giant radios on their shoulders, ultracool. "They're all idiots. Only idiots join the army," Calvin says. "Idiots who can't find any other job except in the army," I reply; he's making me angry. "Sure, sure, they're all soooo underprivileged. If they really wanted to, they could make it, too," he says sharply. "Do you know what you sound like? Like some asshole American." "And you sound like a sentimental German. Just go ahead and declare your solidarity with America's poor downtrodden blacks. Indians, too, of course. Otherwise you'll have a bad conscience. And I wouldn't want you to have a bad conscience. Not as a German." I start to cry. "I'm sorry," he says. "Stop your bawling now."

In the fast-food joint next door we both have a sandwich. The fat German waitress in orthopedic shoes asks us in English if we want mayo or ketchup. A couple of black GIs are sitting around. They stuff themselves with the huge servings, quick and silent, and stare at the TV: "Dallas" in German. The waitress bends over the counter to me. "My own daughter," she says. "My own daughter. With one of them. I should have locked her up. German women have no pride anymore. It was different in the old days. My own daughter. The whole army, nothing but niggers. And they're gonna protect us from the Russians? Niggers are all born sneaks." She jerks her head toward Calvin. "You're lucky. A good-looking man like that."

We leave. The town is black and silent. And it's not even midnight yet. The racket of New York streets roars in my ears. I tell Calvin what the waitress said. "You can hear the same thing word for word in Texas. Or New York. From my grandfather. He hangs up when a receptionist's voice sounds like a black," he says. "That's different," I say. He is silent for two blocks. Then he says, "On our trip today, in that small town, where the fat kid ran across the road in front of us, I saw a little sign with the letters KZ on it. Why didn't you say something to me about it?" "I just couldn't bring myself to," I say. "I'm sorry. I'm so sorry about everything." We turn the corner and suddenly the full moon is hanging over the town. "Calvin?" I say and stop. "Calvin, do you think I love you more than you love me or the other way around?" He doesn't answer. He kisses me. Our kisses taste tired somehow.

My mother has fallen asleep in her armchair. She looks so small and fragile. The dirndl hangs on her as if she were a doll. We startle her. "I was waiting up for you," she says and smooths the apron.

"But, mom, you don't need to do that," I say and

notice how my voice suddenly sounds very weak. "Ah," she says, "it's nice to have someone to wait up for. I haven't had a chance to do it for six years now."

Calvin gives her a goodnight kiss. As we start up the stairs, she pulls me back. I can smell her Joy. Her thin fingers bore into my arm. "I heard you two last night," she says softly, very softly. "What have I ever done to deserve this?" In the dark hallway I can see tears glistening.

Hollywood

I HAD NEVER been in Hollywood before, let alone
to a Hollywood party. A blond guy with a nice tan
named Bobo whom I just met a couple of hours ago
at The Rose, an in place in Venice, dragged me here.
He says he's a producer and is sure Richard Gere is
going to show up at this party. He's got just the right
material for him. Means a movie, I guess. He drives
a Porsche convertible. Shouldn't I change for this
party? I asked him, but he said it wasn't necessary at
all, I looked so sweet and European in my black
leather shorts. I bought them special before I left for
America. Peter, my husband (I really should get used
to calling him my ex-husband, but we're still not of-
ficially divorced), would think they're ghastly, I'm
sure. Peter would never take me along on his business
trips to Lala-land, as he calls it—"You'll just be
bored, believe me." Like a good wife I kept all the
American Express receipts for our tax records—gal-

lons of champagne in the Polo Lounge. Until at some point I was no longer willing to accept his explanation that champagne is definitely standard at American business lunches.

And so here I am alone in Lala-land, thirty-seven years old and almost divorced. But Venice, where I'm living in a small motel on the beach, isn't really part of it, it's just a suburb where everybody hangs around hoping for a ticket to get into the real Lala-land, an invitation to a party like this one.

It's being held in a suite at the Château Marmont. That's a hotel that looks like a cross between a knight's castle and Neuschwanstein; it hovers high above Sunset Boulevard, slapped up on a hill like a sign that reads: DANGER, EUROPE. I already know about the Château Marmont, thanks to the crumpled, almost unreadable yellow American Express receipts I found in Peter's pants pockets. He never stayed here, just spent his (our?) money for "business meetings" here.

From the suite's terrace you can see out over all of Los Angeles. A giant cardboard cowboy pitching Marlboros is so close you can almost touch him. He just casually smokes away. The last smoker in Los Angeles. Only Europe, the Third World, and old, hopeless cowboys still go on poisoning themselves with nicotine.

The red taillights of the cars shine like glowworms down there in the checkerboard of streetlamps. From up here Los Angeles looks like a giant airport for UFOs. Bobo saw some once, in the desert. They flew right over him, real close, three of them.

"They were taking pictures of your Porsche," I say and figure that I've cracked my first good joke in English. He says that's quite possible. Several months ago they found hundreds of cows all hacked to pieces. The Martians had slit open their bellies and taken the organs with them, and that was "a fact."

Richard Gere isn't here yet. I saw him in a movie on German TV, where he dances at the end of the street just before he gets shot. That was a few days after Peter moved out, when only TV and red wine helped me get through the nights.

I really should have changed. I'm conspicuous in my skin-tight black leather shorts and my holey T-shirt. The women are wearing frilly pastel dresses with lots of sewn-on beads, trying for the innocent look and ending up more like call girls. The men have on glittery jackets, like quiz-show emcees. I suddenly feel like some aging hippie mama, when all I really wanted was to take up again where I left off eight years ago at twenty-nine. As an attorney's wife in my Gucci shoes I would have been invisible here, that's for sure. People smile at me with perfectly redesigned

teeth, and I read the only two thoughts that can pos-
sibly lie behind those smiles: What is she doing here?
Either she can afford to get away with it, but then
we'd know her, or she's crashed the party. Bobo has
one of those emcee jackets on now, too; he always
keeps one in his trunk, just in case. A producer has
to be flexible, he says. Waiters in snow-white uniforms
pass around the hors d'oeuvres. Some man near me
says: "No thanks, I'm on a diet." He's as thin as a
matchstick. They are all very thin, very tan, and in
very good shape, and it's hard to guess ages considering the massive cosmetic surgery you can only assume they've had. And they all are talking movies.
They puff little kisses on each other's cheeks, already
smiling at the next person. Phrases like "a very in-
triguing project," "wonderful casting," "brilliant
camerawork" gush out of every buttonhole, while the
eyes search restlessly around the room looking for
celebrities, potential business partners, people they
simply *must* talk to. The women are bored, you can
see that, forcing tortured stupid smiles while their
husbands go hunting, and Bobo is right in there with
them. Although he isn't one of the big-game
hunters—not yet. People move away too quickly,
their eyes start wandering too quickly in search of
more rewarding prey. He comes over to me. "Boring
party," he says, "nobody but agents, lawyers, and

managers." And as he says this he looks over the top of my head and his eyes suddenly catch fire. A small, gray-haired man has arrived, I see him for just a fraction of a second, then he is surrounded by party guests.

"He's here," Bobo whispers, "Richard Gere's agent. That means Richard will be here soon!" He jumps up and joins the group around Richard Gere's agent; they look like people waiting in line outside a department store. The telephone rings, but no one seems to notice.

Since it's right beside me, I finally pick it up. A woman's voice says: "Do you ski?" "Sometimes," I say. "Who was it you wanted to speak with?" "Someone who skis, of course." I address the room loudly. "Somebody on the telephone wants to speak to a skier." Everyone stops talking and stares at me. A woman about forty with a sunburned cleavage titters and says to me: "Don't you ski?" "Well," I say, "now and then. In the Alps." The whole party breaks into uproarious laughter. "In the Alps" they gasp, "did you hear, 'in the Alps'!" Bobo comes to my rescue. He picks up the receiver and says, "Listen, there's only one lady here, and she skis in the Alps. I'm afraid I have to disappoint you otherwise." Another wave of laughter breaks, a man buckles over with glee and has to hold on to a chair. I can see Richard Gere's agent again now, but suddenly he seems to be of no interest, they have all turned away from him to look at Bobo. Bobo casts a proud glance all around. He puts a hand over the receiver and says, "A lady in the room next door is on the phone. She wants to know if anyone wants to join her for some skiing." The woman with the sunburned bosom cries, "Why don't we send our Alpine skier over!" Bobo says to the telephone, "Would you be interested in a lady who only skis in the Alps?" The laughter falls away; they all watch Bobo intently. He puts his hand over the receiver again. "She'd prefer a man who skis." "Hoho," Richard Gere's short agent bellows in a bass that is amazingly deep for his size. "Now this is getting interesting. A man! Any particulars as to age, profession, or income?" Bobo asks the telephone, "Do you have a more precise idea of what kind of man it is you want?," and after a longish pause, which leaves the guests simply quivering with curiosity, he tells the telephone, "We'll see," and hangs up. "Around thirty, well-built guy, surfer type," he reports. "About like you," an especially thin, trim woman calls out, and that's true, that's just what Bobo looks like, and suddenly they're all shouting, "Right, you've got to do it!" "Oh, please!" "Come on, do us a favor!" "Go on over and then tell us about it!" Bobo waves this off with a laugh. "I don't even ski," he says. "None of us do," a man with a shiny bald head says, and they all giggle. "You have to go! Who knows, maybe we'll see the plot of a whole new movie this evening." And the short agent adds, "The opening isn't all that bad: A party. A call. A woman in the next room wants a man." "To go skiing!" someone else contributes. "Sure, sure," a woman in lavender says cattily. "And who gets the rights to our movie?" a man calls out, his face so shriveled he looks like a baked apple. "Mac," the agent says, "that'll be the most complicated contract in your legal career."

"Go for it," the thin trim woman says to Bobo, "go on." Bobo gives an embarrassed grin and then actually does it. The guests form a pathway to the door, and just before he leaves the room Bobo turns around again, the way all American actors do in films to deliver their exit lines, and says, "But I want the franchise rights," and apparently it was a good punch line, because they all laugh. The baked apple comes over to me. "So, you ski in the Alps," and smirks. "Would you be kind enough to explain what all this skiing thing is all about?" I ask him, and he starts screaming with laughter, so that they all turn around to me again, and he has trouble getting it out. "The lady here wants to know what this skiing thing is all about." The skinny exercise freak asks me where I'm from, and her reply to my answer is "Germany, oh I see. Then you really don't know. I thought you were turning it into a really terrific joke." "The part with the Alps had real class," the baked apple says and then whispers in my ear, "Skiing means snorting coke."

They all watch as I finally catch on. Richard Gere's agent bellows, "But it's actually quite refreshing to meet someone who really does ski in the Alps," and now a group has formed around me and I'm apparently supposed to tell them about the Alps and cuckoo clocks and Swiss chocolate. But before I can get around to it, the door opens and Bobo's back. "I need a drink," he says, and someone brings him one. Like children listening to a fairytale, they all hang on his lips. Bobo pauses for effect. "Well," he says slowly. "Get to the action!" Richard Gere's agent shouts.

"Well, now," Bobo says, "it's a couple. The man a little on the heavy side, bald, but good-looking." "More details!" someone yells. "She's in her early thirties, red hair, nice figure," Bobo goes on. "They're both—naked. All she's wearing is a pearl necklace. A long pearl necklace. Genuine, I'd say. They're bored. They're looking for a third." Bobo's audience sighs softly in suspense. "And?" asks the woman in lavender. Bobo shrugs. "But that won't do," the thin woman says. "We want to know what happens next."

"Just a minute," Bobo objects.

"Right, we want to know what happens next!" two women shout in chorus, both dressed alike as if they're twins, and giggling excitedly. "Yes, yes, yes!" the burned bosom screeches. The women suddenly start acting as if they're at a boarding-school slumber party. They circle around Bobo, who is obviously flattered, begging him to go back next door. "You simply must!" I hear one of them say. "Otherwise it's just the trailer for the big movie." By chance I catch the amazed look on her husband's face.

The men have all backed off politely now. They are still smiling, but they are no longer sure of themselves. And suddenly I realize why the women are in such a tizzy. They recognize the opening scenes of this movie: a man says goodnight to his wife, he has to go to one of those dreadfully boring business dinners, "Honey, I may be late, just go on to bed. You don't know how lucky you are not to have to go." And they know the ending, too: the credit-card bills for champagne and an expensive dinner. But maybe Bobo can tell them what really happens in the middle. And right in front of their husbands! Like a kid spilling family secrets. One rather nondescript woman in a cloud of pink organdy presses a bottle of Moët et Chandon into Bobo's hand, and Bobo realizes the high price of suddenly standing in the center of Hollywood's illustrious few. He can't quit now.

He stands up, looks around with a foolish little smile, and can't seem to come up with the appropriate wisecrack. "Well, then," he says. He has no sooner left the room than the cloud of pink organdy comes floating over to me, "What's your friend's name?" she asks. She barely waits for my answer to ask the really important question: "And what is it he does?" "He's a producer," I say. Her mouth, so heavily painted with gloss it looks like lips in aspic, immediately lifts in an ironic smile. "Oh, is that right?" she says and is about to turn away when her husband comes over and puts his arm around her shoulder. She turns back to me as if we had been deep in conversation and says, "And you just let your friend go off like that? Ah, well, at least he does it out in the open, right?" Her husband takes his arm off her shoulder as if he's been burned and pretends he has to look for his drink. I have served my purpose, and the organdy cloud floats off again. Suddenly I'm aware that I am the only woman in the room without a man, that all at once couples have formed. There are very obviously married couples everywhere. The husbands come to heel beside their wives as if to say, "Listen here, surely you don't think I've ever done anything like that. Not me." The few men who have come to the party alone and I are suddenly excluded.

We are loosely scattered around the room, occupying its corners and thanking our lucky stars that we don't have to play this game. I can suddenly feel Peter beside me, the way he lays his hand on the back of my neck and says, "Me? You don't have to worry about that with me. I have you, don't I? And I really don't find American women all that attractive."

As if shot from a cannon, Bobo returns, and the couples immediately break up, the women make a dash for him, someone hands him a drink, he drops into an armchair.

"She wanted me to whip her with her pearl necklace," he blurts out. "And did you do it?" two women ask at once. Bobo says nothing. The women are watching him eagerly; the men shift their weight uneasily from one foot to the other. The atmosphere in the room is explosive, all it will take is a match. The thin woman provides it. In a loud, clear voice she says, "Does anyone have a condom?" The men laugh, the loud and long laughter of professionals in a sitcom; the women squeal, "A condom! A condom!" Bobo turns red and pours himself another drink. And since it is perfectly clear that no one here is going to admit he has one on him, the organdy cloud shrieks, "Then we'll call room service!" and strides to the telephone. "You can't do that," her husband says and masks this with a giggle. "It's the eighties, isn't it?" the thin woman cries. The organdy cloud's husband takes the receiver from her hand. "You can't do that to him," he says, pointing to Bobo, who has slumped in his chair and is staring glassy-eyed into space. The women look at him expectantly. If he backs out now he'll be punished by having to spend the next ten years on Venice beach. Or is he going to fight for his place in the history of Hollywood parties as the man who . . . ? "I have a condom," Bobo says. And all female heads swing my way as if this were a tennis match; some eyes are filled with pity for me. Bobo pulls a condom out of his pocket and lays it on the table. He looks around the room like a magician before he pulls the white rabbit from his top hat, and very slowly says, "It'll cost you." Aha, a genuine inhabitant of Lala-land. The women clap rapturously, the men suddenly regard Bobo with respect, business is business, and smiles flash for a fraction of a second. The burned bosom picks up a vase of roses, dumps its contents out on the terrace, and places the empty vase on the carpet in front of Bobo. "What are the stakes?" she asks him. "A hundred dollars!" she shouts like an auctioneer. "A hundred dollars!"

The organdy cloud rummages in her purse and tosses the first bill into the vase. She is greeted with furious applause. But she is apparently the only woman present with her own cash, and so the wives hurry over to their husbands, who pull their wallets out with embarrassed grins. They have no choice. They must either pay up or argue with their wives. They all pay. The vase fills up with green bills. Bobo beams. He had explained the ground rules of success to me this afternoon: If you really want to make it, you have to be ready to eat shit. He is about to stick the money in his pocket, but the organdy cloud pulls the vase away, presses it to her bosom, and coolly declares, "Payment upon delivery of the screenplay."

The women screech with delight, their husbands— the lawyers, agents, and managers—laugh politely. Someone pours Bobo one for the road. With almost maternal solicitude the woman in lavender slips the condom into his pocket. The thin one breaks into a kind of football cheer, hopping up and down, her aerobically disciplined breasts hopping reluctantly in sync. The other women join in.

And Bobo turns around one last time before pulling the door closed. He waves as only an American can wave, a semicircle with his whole arm that comes to an abrupt halt.

I pick up the roses on the terrace. There are no thorns. No one notices when I leave.

Sunset Boulevard is deserted. People go to bed early in Hollywood. I wander past the exclusive restaurants, a few street cafés, where in the middle of Los Angeles you can pretend you're in Rome or Paris. The

Marlboro man glows in the distance. Cars pass, humming softly. The passengers turn their heads to look at me. Finally a Mercedes convertible pulls up. The driver is about thirty, blond and tanned. He gives me a ride to Venice. "So you're from Europe," he says. "I thought so. Only whores and Europeans walk in this town."

"Let me guess what you do," I say. "You're a producer." He looks at me dumbfounded.

"How did you know that?" he says.

Los Angeles

"THE WHITE ZONE is for loading and unloading only." Even with her eyes closed she would have been able to tell where she was from that single sentence constantly repeated over the loudspeaker. LAX, the Los Angeles airport. The limousine drivers held up signs with the names of their fares, families hugged, young men shyly held out a few flowers to their arriving girlfriends.

She hadn't expected Dave to pick her up, but all the same she had quickly added a little lipstick and rouge before going through customs.

The air was warm, like a day with foehn wind back home. It had snowed in Frankfurt. "The white zone is for loading and unloading only." She was standing right under the speaker. She recognized several of the passengers who were loading their bags into the cars picking them up. The woman who had sat next to her, and who looked as flawless now after twelve hours in a plane as she had in Frankfurt—fresh, not a hair out of place, wearing heels—gave a tall blond man a quick hug and climbed into a black Mercedes.

Marie stuck a peppermint into her mouth. Just in case Dave showed up after all. She felt sticky and tired.

Three days ago on the phone he had said, "I'm looking forward to seeing you." That meant he'd really be glad, right? . . .

"Call me if you happen to be in Los Angeles." And by chance she was in Los Angeles, quite by chance. As much by chance as a twenty-two-year-old technical draftsperson from Hamburg could be. She had taken unpaid vacation, plundered her savings, bought two new summer dresses, signed up for a crash course in English, just to be here quite by chance.

She had carefully studied a Falz map of Los Angeles and had drawn a circle with a red marker around his address. He lived on the beach. Or almost on the beach.

She wondered if she should call him. "Just by chance I'm at the airport. . . ." And then he would pick her up and she would fall asleep right there in his car.

She decided to take a bus to his part of the city, to stretch out on the beach, sleep a little, and then, just by chance, give him a call.

She wandered the airport, her pack on her back. Her feet were hot, her socks were much too warm. She noticed she was starting to stink from head to toe. She asked several people about the bus to Santa Monica—two spoke no English, she didn't understand the black guy, a fourth one pointed vaguely in the direction of the other end of the airport.

Three Chinese people were standing all alone with their baggage under a bus-stop sign, and she joined them. Ten minutes passed, and Marie asked: "Santa Monica? Santa Monica?" The three Chinese nodded.

The bus driver wouldn't accept the dollar bill she tried to hand him and instead nodded his head at a plastic box full of change. "How much?" Marie asked and without looking at her the driver said, "No bills." The Chinese waiting patiently behind her finally changed her dollar for her, pointed at the plastic box, threw in seventy-five cents, and gave her twenty-five cents back. Marie was suddenly close to tears.

She put her pack on her lap and held her face against the wind pressing like puffy cottonballs through the open window. There wasn't a single American among the passengers, or at least no one who matched Marie's idea of one. No one was tall and blond and tanned like Dave, no one had his American teeth, that broad smile with healthy, white teeth, which for Marie was the hallmark of all Americans.

They rode past endless rows of small Spanish-style houses. The well-tended yards had flowers Marie didn't recognize, and there were clean, bright-colored cars parked in front. There was no one on the street, and all she could hear was the soft sound of sprinklers.

Marie's mood grew light and merry. She recognized all this from the countless TV series that flickered across the screen at home in Hamburg, evening after evening, when she sat down to a cozy meal of spaghetti and wine after work. More recently to cottage cheese and tomatoes, because Dave had talked about her "European figure," and she assumed that what he meant was plump.

He had asked her for directions on Jungfernstieg, and two beers later had gone with her to her place. He had lain in her bed seven times. And then he had said: "Call me."

Four times she had secretly used her boss's telephone to call Los Angeles after the office closed. And every time he said he missed her. And she said: "I miss you, too."

She woke up when the bus driver gave her a poke. As she got out she saw the ocean. With a long row of straggly palm trees in front. An autobahn lay between Marie and the Pacific. Highway One. She walked to the nearest telephone. She knew the American dial tone from movies. And the sound of how

American telephones ring. Just like the telephone now at Dave's apartment—or house?—would sound.

"Hello," a man's voice said. And the asphalt gave way under Marie. "It's me. Marie."

His voice sounded so close; there was no roar of the Atlantic between them. He asked how she was doing, she kept saying, "Fine, fine," he explained how he had wanted to call her but had been pretty "busy," and then he said, "You're not in bed yet?" Well, she was kind of tired, she replied, and he laughed and suggested that most anybody would be at three in the morning. Only now did it occur to her.

"I'm here. Here in Los Angeles."

"Oh," he said. Then there was a pause. The palm trees swayed. A man in sweats ran past. The Pacific murmured in the distance. Dave suggested a meeting four days later. "Call me at six." Marie said, "Fine."

She hung up and it started to rain. It poured, a cold wind suddenly swept over her, she ran up and down the street looking for a bar, a shop, some refuge. There was nothing.

Long palm fronds fell on the sidewalk ahead of her. There was water in her shoes. The man came jogging past her again. His pastel sweats were dark and soggy now. He turned around to look at her. Marie just stood there. Maybe Dave had mistaken who she was. Maybe someone had been in the room, and he hadn't wanted him to know about her. Or her, hadn't wanted her to know? He had told her in Hamburg, after the first beer, that he was divorced.

There were three hotels on this street, each about a half mile from the next. Their prices far exceeded Marie's means. The desk clerks were friendly and noticed the puddles forming on the carpet around Marie's feet.

When she came out onto the street after hotel number three, it was getting dark and the rain had stopped.

Marie hurt all over. She trudged back to the bus stop. There wasn't another soul on the street. She would try to find a cheap hotel near the airport. Her teeth were chattering, her whole body was shaking.

She jumped up and down and spun about in circles to warm herself. On the other side of the street she spotted a defunct neon sign, only three letters of which were still lit: THE . . . The rest was swallowed in the darkness. THE GEORGIAN she was able to make out once she stood there in front of the little, somewhat ramshackle building. She opened the front door and breathed a sigh of relief. It was a hotel. The lobby had red wallpaper and tattered red chairs arranged in a tidy row. She walked down the worn red carpet, although she couldn't see anyone at the poorly lit reception desk. And there was no one there, either.

But there was a big bell on the counter. But when Marie rang it the sound made her flinch.

A clerk bent with age and wearing a blue uniform came out of a back room, took a hard look at her, and shook his head.

He spoke with a thick accent. "We don't rent rooms."

"Isn't this a hotel?" Marie asked.

"Yes. It's a very fine hotel, in fact," the clerk said, holding tight to the counter with both hands as if he would topple over otherwise.

"It's full?"

"Almost."

"Then you do have rooms available?"

"Yes," he said, "but we don't rent them out."

"I desperately need a room. For four days."

The old man looked at her calmly.

"Where are you from?" he asked.

"From Germany. I just arrived today . . ."

"Ach," the old man said now in German, "from Germany."

"Yes," Marie said, shifting impatiently from one foot to the other, "and I need a room."

"Mein liebes Fräulein," he spoke slowly, stressing each word, "this is a hotel for old people, not young ones."

Marie looked at him uncomprehendingly. And he went into a long-winded but friendly explanation of how this was a kind of old folks' home and that for years now no young person had wandered in here by mistake. Besides, they only rented by the month, and as much as he would like to, there was no way he could give her a room for four days. . . .

After a little give-and-take, Marie rented a room for one week, at the same price one night would have cost in the other hotels that she had worked her way through.

The elevator was padded and had several handrails about hip high.

"Goodnight, mein Fräulein," the clerk said. She was unsure whether to tip him, and so didn't.

The room was practically an apartment, with kitchen, living room, bed and dressing rooms. Marie smiled for the first time since she had arrived in Los Angeles.

She woke up at three in morning, saw the moon and panicked. It was lying on its back. Incredulous, she went to the window. It was still lying on its back; it looked all wrong. Marie stared at this wrong-way moon, thought of Dave, and wondered if the moon might be shining wrong side up in his room, too. Just before she fell asleep again she realized that it was because of the equator, the rotation of the earth . . . it felt a little bit like being drunk.

By seven the next morning the sun was shining the way it is supposed to shine in California, and Marie was no longer sure whether she had seen the moon wrong side up or not, or had just dreamed it.

She was hungry and asked at the desk where the breakfast room was. The night clerk had been relieved by another, equally old man, who stared at her in disbelief and then pointed the way with an outstretched arm.

The breakfast room was in the basement, its wallpaper the same red as the lobby's. A small lamp was lit on every table. Shyly Marie took a seat on a leather chair. She was surrounded by old people. One old woman was holding a doll in her arm, talking to it softly. An old man was shoving a metal frame in front of him, step by step.

The waiter who came to her table, however, was a mere child in comparison, fifty at most. His face brightened when he saw Marie.

"Visiting?" he asked. Marie nodded because she found it especially difficult to speak English in the morning.

"I wish I was just visiting here," the waiter said, sighing. "I assume you still have your teeth and you don't want oatmeal or Cream of Wheat or bread without crusts. How would you like some toast, eggs, and a big order of bacon?"

Marie nodded. "And coffee," she said softly.

"Coffee with caffeine!" the waiter proclaimed loudly and disappeared.

The woman with the doll sighed and whispered across the table, "She doesn't want to eat anything today." Marie gave her a nod.

Later she wandered down deserted streets toward the red circle she had marked on her map. After an hour it seemed further away than at the start. A police car stopped beside her. "What's your problem?" the policemen asked. She was close to telling them about Dave. She had to show them her passport, which convinced the police that her only obvious problem was that she was a foreigner.

After three hours, during which Marie had not passed a single shop and Dave's address was as far away as the North Pole, she sat down on a patch of grass in the middle of the street and wished with all her heart for a car.

A woman standing in her yard watering flowers yelled something to her. Marie stood up and walked toward her. The woman dropped the hose and ran into the house.

The TV in her room was kaput. The Pacific, ice cold. There was the book she had taken along for the flight, but she had read that twice already.

The elevator operator, a thin man in his sixties, confided to her that he hated old people and ran three miles every day.

The second day she sat in the lobby and gazed silently out to sea. Between breakfast and lunch they all sat there staring mutely out to sea. A couple of women knitted or read magazines, two men played chess, most of them sat there motionless, staring at the Pacific and waiting.

For the hundredth time Marie ran through her mind all the possible explanations of why Dave hadn't wanted to see her for four days. Not one of them made any sense. Not after his declarations of love in Hamburg, words she had never heard from any man before. She asked herself if she had misunderstood them all, because they had been in English. But then she must have misunderstood his body, too, and God knows there was no way of misunderstanding that. But then what is a body?

The old woman dressed her doll in a bathing suit. At half past noon they all got up and shuffled into the dining room. Marie stayed behind alone and cried a little.

She tried twice more to lie out on the beach, so that

she at least could take a little tan back to her office in Hamburg, but every time she closed her eyes despair covered her like a black towel, and she decided she would do her waiting in the company of others and sit with the old people in the hotel lobby. The palm trees, the flowers, and the sun, the relaxed faces rolling silently by in shiny cars—they only magnified her unhappiness. She could have borne the rain and wind of the first day better than the constant demand to be happy imposed by this permanently lovely weather.

There was a pay telephone hanging in the hall, and every day she played with the thought of calling Dave again. But she didn't know what she should say. And maybe the telephone didn't even work, no one ever used it.

She woke up at six on the morning of the fourth day, her heart pounding. Her unhappiness was forgotten. This evening at six, just as she had promised, she would call him, she would see him, he would ask her forgiveness and say, "I missed you." She washed her hair, shaved her legs, laid out different combinations of clothes on her bed, decided to decide later which one to wear, just as the mood struck her. She even risked going back to the gloomy breakfast room, which she had avoided since that first morning, and

when the waiter once again trumpeted his loud chal-
lenge of "Coffee with caffeine" to the old people, she
just smiled.

In the lobby she gave a friendly nod to the woman
with the doll, took her seat—after the first day it had
become *her* seat, always unoccupied until she
arrived—and waited patiently, minute after minute.
As the sky slowly began to turn red—it was after
five—a young man burst in. The old people slowly
turned their heads, watching as he talked briefly to
the clerk and then went to the pay telephone. He
shifted his weight impatiently from one leg to the
other, then screamed into the phone: "But I love you!
How could you do this to me!" They all stared at him
in mute surprise, some of them put hands to their ears
to hear better.

"You think you can just forget four years! I'm begging you, come back! Do you hear? I can't live without
you!" the young man shouted, and Marie had heard
all these phrases a hundred times on TV, felt she knew
them all by heart. No one in the lobby could take his
eyes off the young man, every head was turned, every
ear listened eagerly.

"I'd do anything, anything. You can't simply forget
it all, forget four years!"

The young man didn't seem to notice the eyes fixed

on him. His voice kept getting louder and louder, and he punctuated his desperation with big and pathetic gestures.

"But I love you!" he shouted, then hung up, stood there motionless for a brief moment, before leaving as swiftly as he had arrived, hurried down the red runner, and vanished.

The old people's heads followed him all the way to the door, its bell tinkled, and then everything was quiet again. They all went on looking out to sea.

When Marie stood there at ten after six with the pay-phone receiver in her damp, sweaty hand, she turned her face to the wall and spoke as softly as she could. He was terribly sorry, Dave said, but his mother had arrived in the meantime, and he had to look after her; she was an old lady who made lots of demands, and couldn't he see her next week maybe? He could definitely make it then. He really was dreadfully sorry, as he'd said, but that was the way his mother always did things, just showed up and expected him to look after her like a little kid. She didn't want to spend a minute alone, didn't Marie feel sorry for him with a mother like that? At the end he said, "Have fun." And Marie said softly, "Yes."

When she hung up and turned around she saw how the old people were sitting there immobile, watching her over the backs of their chairs. The doll sat straddling a pillow and its head wobbled. Marie took two steps forward, the heads were about to turn back to the ocean, the old woman had taken the doll down and was kissing it. But then Marie wheeled around and ran to the elevator. Once again they all turned to watch her.

"Oh, how I hate them all. Old people," the elevator operator said to her.

A Man!

EVER SINCE that newspaper article claiming New York women over thirty have a better chance of being hit by an atom bomb than of finding a husband, I can see the panic in the faces of my American friends. The probability of being hit by an atom bomb is really rather good, I try to reassure them, so it can't be so bad when it comes to husbands. Yes, in Europe maybe, they reply, but not here in America. Since I am thirty-three years old, have lived in New York for five years now, and have no intention of returning to Germany just because the threat of atomic war and, apparently, the statistical chances of catching a husband are greater there, I have begun to give the matter serious thought.

I've been separated from Johannes for three years now. More and more he missed German beer and stew—he called it "culture"—and went back to Hamburg. I've thought of him often ever since I read that stupid article. He has made his mark as a fashion photographer in Germany. After our separation I sometimes dropped by Bremenhaus on Eighty-sixth Street to page through the fashion spreads in German women's magazines and steamed with jealousy every time I caught a model making eyes at the photographer, at Johannes. Today, for instance, I spot his name in fine print under the latest collection in *Brigitte*. The models look more bored than anything else. No, it wasn't a mistake to let him go. But at the time, three years ago, I didn't know anything about the connection between atom bombs and men and women over thirty.

Just like old times, I buy a piece of Tilsit from the woman at the cheese counter because I love to hear her speak English with a Saxon accent. The sign over the counter says: QUARK TODAY.

The Tilsit is stinking away there in my purse, and I'm sitting here in the Kleine Konditorei, poking at a piece of Black Forest cake and asking myself (a) did I really think I'd find an acceptable husband in here of all places and (b) do I really want to find a husband? The more I watch the blue-haired old ladies all around me, the way they lustily shovel away at their Linzer tortes and cream cakes, complaining about the weather and their health, the more I envy them. They have outlived their husbands, but I'll never find another one.

Actually I've not really missed a man in my life since Johannes left.

Sometimes when I felt like a little sex would do me, my creativity, and my complexion some good, I had brief affairs, but since that's no longer safe I've discovered that a shopping spree at the Chanel boutique has about the same effect. My drawings improve immediately, I feel better, and my skin looks much smoother, too. Long live Chanel.

I already regret the Black Forest cake. I feel sick at my stomach, unhealthy, a prey to instinct, un-American. I stopped eating red meat and drinking coffee months ago, gave up smoking years ago, keep a close watch on my cholesterol level, am careful not to take in too much sodium, never drink alcohol, get my exercise, and try hard, like any real American, to believe that you can make it if you really want to. For three years now I've been going once a week to a psychotherapist, who reinforces that belief and issues emphatic warnings about getting trapped in a relationship, all for a hundred twenty dollars an hour. And so I've moved up the ladder. In New York. And I've got my co-op in the Village, too. So why do I suddenly want a husband?

I can't ask my therapist that now, not after three years. Those are beginner's issues. All her efforts would have been in vain.

How does one go about finding a husband? Ever since the gruesome statistics were first published, women's magazines have been loaded with tips and suggestions. The column is called: "Never Be Lonely Again: How Clever Cosmo Girls Meet Men," and readers tell how they've pulled it off. (What is a Cosmo Girl? Am I one? I'll just assume I am.) Penelope, stewardess, twenty-eight years old, writes: "Men will often start talking to you if you are lugging around some strange object. Of course you should pick out something that really interests you, otherwise the conversation is over in a few seconds. I've had good luck with a huge iron cross." Interesting. Penelope's suggestion has only one crucial defect. She is only twenty-eight, and statistics say she doesn't even need that iron cross of hers. I'm more inclined to trust Barbara, TV producer, thirty-six years old: "Take a real good look around where you work. The trick is to pick out someone all the other women aren't already working on. Of course, you should like him, too."

Well, now, Barbara, in my editorial office there's only the boss, whom all the women are working on, and an itty-bitty hunchback layout man with thick glasses. I like him, no question of that, but I am three years younger than you, my dear Barbara, and I'm not that far gone (yet).

Judy, however, tax consultant, is exactly the same age as I am, thirty-three. She writes: "I often meet men in department stores. Some especially recommended departments: leather goods, stationery, and electronics. Don't even think of ambushing him in men's clothing. Every man will assume you're there looking for a shirt for your boyfriend. The same goes for women's underwear. Housewares are good, men are so helpless there." I'm a little skeptical about her claim that she "often" meets men in this fashion. How many rejects were there? But it seems worth a try.

For four days now I've gone to Macy's after work, but in all the departments Judy so warmly recommends I didn't see a single man, only women. I suspect they are all there for the same reason I am. We slink around like cats, watching one another as we finger the wallets and suitcases, try out mixers and toasters, or let salespeople demonstrate a typewriter for hours on end, and almost never buying anything, and if we do, only by way of camouflage. Our glances skitter restlessly over the shelves. At the same time we give each other a hostile once-over and try to guess each other's age. How much over thirty?

A Man!

But today at Bloomingdale's, maybe my horoscope was favorable, I was suddenly all alone in leather goods, and a man about forty emerged from behind a pigskin suitcase, like a deus ex machina. A man with thick, light brown hair, good-looking, maybe a tiny bit too serious for my taste, but I can't afford such quibbles anymore at my age. So there he was, standing by the suitcases, snapping them open and shut, and I sidled nearer, slowly and as inconspicuously as possible, through wallets and women's purses, until I was standing almost next to him, and then I heard him tell the salesman he was looking for as elegant a suitcase as possible; he made a lot of business trips and usually had to go directly from the airport to his meeting. My heart sank right then and there. What good is a husband in whose suit jacket I would someday be sure to find the telephone numbers of Monique in Paris or Gabi in Stuttgart?

Instead, I bought myself the latest issue with "How Clever Cosmo Girls Meet Men." In this one, Susanne, dental assistant, thirty-five, writes: "My ex-husband didn't like dogs, so we bought a rabbit instead. When we got divorced I got custody of the rabbit. I always take it along on the train to Connecticut. A whole lot of interesting men have sat down beside me just to pet the rabbit."

I suddenly have a violent longing for a little black rabbit with white ears, but my parents live in Wuppertal and not in Connecticut. Where am I supposed to go with my rabbit? I can see myself, alone and forlorn, in the New Haven station some night, the last train for New York has already left, and far and wide not one interesting man in sight who wants to pet my rabbit.

Of late I've been daydreaming, too. I see a man cracking open his breakfast egg in my kitchen, or a different one sitting on my couch, martini in hand, or there's one standing under the shower, or I discover one in my bed. He looks up at me eagerly and smiles.

My therapist notices I've developed a facial tic. She thinks I'm a bundle of negative energy. I've been coming to that same office every Wednesday at eleven for three years now, and there's always a whiff of aftershave in the air, the couch is still warm from the previous occupant. Sometimes if I'm early and have to sit in the waiting room I can hear his sonorous voice. But I've never actually seen him yet. My therapist, being a discreet woman, has her patients leave by a different door before the next one is allowed in. I found his voice especially sympathetic today.

"Exercise," my therapist says. "Exercise?" I ask

weakly. For two years now I've been going to the gym every other day. She prescribes a vacation.

I take four weeks off. Without the daily routine of work, the absence of a man is all the more painful. I ring up all my girlfriends. I'm a little wary of them all since reading the article about having to stalk down a husband. "You know," Margie, thirty-six, says, "since I read those damned statistics all I see in the mirror is a woman with cellulite and a slipped disc, with no husband, no double bed, and no pension." I accuse her of being materialistic, and she calls me an incorrigible European romantic. She wants to advertise for a man as a roommate to share her tiny two-bedroom apartment. "There's an average of four hundred inquiries in response to every ad," Margie says, "and whoever finally finds a room in Manhattan never moves out." "Unless he marries somebody else," I object. Offended, she hangs up.

Unfortunately my apartment has only one bedroom. But if I'd extend a wall through the living room. . . . There'd have to be one acceptable applicant among those four hundred.

The movie on TV, as always when I'm not doing well, is *The Way We Were*. Ah, Barbra Streisand, nowadays you wouldn't be able to afford the luxury of breaking up with Robert Redford just because you don't agree on politics.

In college there were a lot of men who looked like Redford: ruggedly handsome, with fabulous teeth and unshakable optimism. Where are they all now? Not in New York at any rate. I bet they're all married, and that after reading the story about atom bomb–husband statistics, their wives breathed sighs of relief as they ironed their shirts and whooped when they brought them beers. Why did I have to fall in love with the only German at college, of all people? Johannes wore nicer underwear, snug briefs, not those ghastly boxer shorts; he smoked and talked about art, he was different from the Americans, he was like me, back then.

I don't expect the love of my life. I just want to watch a man shave in the morning, watch baseball on TV with him and pretend it interests me. I don't want to go on making up my double bed on both sides just in case, I want to find Budweiser in the fridge and aftershave in the bathroom, to lie with him on a towel at the beach and hear him tell me I've got a better figure than the other women. Is that too much to ask? Streisand is still handing out her flyers when she sees Bobby again years later, and they still love each other, but all the same they can't ever get together, not ever, and I cry at the end just like always. Damn it all, I want to feel the real pain of love again sometime.

A Man!

In the *Village Voice* there's a supplement for summer courses, including ones in Creative Hypnosis, The Secret of Charisma, The Power of Crystals, Make Miracles Happen Through the Power of Love, and How to Build a Greeting-Card Business.

You can also take sightseeing tours of the homes of famous movie stars, or the sites of famous murders, or both as a special discount offer. I briefly consider signing up, but you'd probably meet only tourists, and you've no more than got the telephone number down by heart, when they're on their way home. There are, to be sure, courses made to order for my problem: 52 Ways to Find a Lover, The Creative Flirt, and for advanced students The Creative Relationship. But somehow I—still—resist the idea of taking a course where people use role play to practice creative flirting with others just as unsuccessful at it as they are. As if I were too stupid to flirt. When she would spot a particularly strange couple, my mother always said, "There's no pot so dented that a lid won't fit." I ask myself if I'm the pot or the lid.

My friend Julie calls me and reports excitedly about how she's now going to Alcoholics Anonymous meetings every day; you can meet all kinds of interesting men there. "But you've never so much as sniffed alcohol," I say. "You've got to be willing to make sacrifices," she says. "I drink a bottle of beer every day now, sometimes even two. I have to be able to contribute, after all. And you know I'm slowly developing a taste for it!" She giggles happily.

I pull out my bottle of whiskey, the one my co-workers in the office gave me for my birthday a year ago and that has stood unopened in the cupboard since then. I drink it in little swallows like medicine. I don't know if I could get used to it or not, but there is a Smokers Anonymous, too. For the first time in two years I have an urge for a cigarette.

I take a pillow and the whiskey bottle and lean out the window. For every handsome man who passes, I make a mark on the window frame, a cross for every semi-attractive one. I don't count the ones over fifty or under twenty. After three hours 187 men have passed beneath my window, 53 of them in the company of women, 3 really handsome and 7 semi-attractive. Depressing percentages. Down on the street a derelict is dragging a cardboard box behind him. "If you ask me just once more if I love you, if you ask me just one more time . . ." he says to his box.

I down half the bottle. Five men are sitting on my couch and ask me if I love them.

I leave the apartment.

On Sixth Avenue a palm reader is sitting at a folding table. She waves to me and yells, "Your future is in your hand!" I'm sure my hand reads: "Joke's on you. No man in sight."

I pass the cheap, musty Chinese restaurant where Johannes and I spent our last evening before he flew back to Germany. "You can always come later," he said. Maybe he should have said, "Come with me. Please." When you really need some useful piece of Chinese philosophy you always find the tritest crap in your fortune cookie. That evening mine said: "Big events don't make big noises."

A new shop has opened up next to the Chinese restaurant, the Magic Center. In the window are nice tidy rows of spray cans to fight off "negative energy" or "envy and malice," little bottles labeled "I-Am-Strong Oil" and "Come-Hither Oil." Under the influence of my own bottled courage, I head straight into the shop and explain my problem to the two fellows who are selling magic, both in black leather and hung with heavy chains and plastic skulls. They listen with the same gentle smiles and encouraging nods my psychotherapist uses. But all in vain! They are obviously gay, which doesn't make it any easier for me to unburden myself. What woman gladly admits she's too stupid to find a man. "No need for self-recriminations," one of them says to me, the one with a carrot-red tonsure. "Have you read the statistics that say it is more likely for a woman over thirty to get hit by an atom bomb?" I nod bitterly. "Simply dreadful," the other one says. "But there are just as many men as women, aren't there?" I ask. "Well, yes," they both say in unison and look at each other. "There are still enough straights," the redhead says turning to me, "they're just hard to find. It's a little bit like with . . . with dogs. . . ." "Horses," the other one says. "Yes, like with horses," the redhead continues, casting his companion a tender smile. "If you run after them they just gallop off that much faster. You have to just stand there and send out positive vibrations." And that's why they highly recommend I try their Come-Hither Package, consisting of Come-Hither Oil, a sachet of love scent that you always have to wear, and a candle I'm supposed to engrave with the name of the man I desire. "But I don't have anyone definite in mind," I say timidly.

This causes them both to rock their heads doubtfully. In this town anonymous magic was to be avoided at all cost, there were too many crazies out there who were highly receptive to magic. "And then you'd never get rid of them." They urgently advise me to seek out one specific victim (at the mention of "victim" the red-tonsured fellow gives his friend a gentle, reproving poke in the ribs), to make a note of his name, rip out one of his hairs or examine his jacket for one that has fallen out, and then proceed with the charm as per instructions.

I buy the Come-Hither Package. They are quick to help hang the sachet of love scent around my neck, because sometimes just its odor alone is enough, and send me on my way with their best wishes and exhortations to think positively. The sachet gives off the penetrating odor of musk.

My therapist declares she can smell negative vibrations. She has attended a seminar in how to detect the odors of psychological disturbances, an old Chinese science, and while she is telling me about it I suddenly spot a long gray hair on her couch. I carefully pick it off and slip it into my wallet.

"And above all, don't try to cure your depression with a relationship," she impresses on me as I leave. As she turns to open the door I cast a quick glance at the schedule on her desk: "10 A.M., L. MONTE-LEONE" is just ahead of me at eleven. L. Monteleone, the sonorous voice. A gray-haired, handsome Italian, in his early forties, an artist maybe, for whom the world is too much, or so I imagine him, and look in my wallet right away—the hair is still there—or a fat mafia boss in a camel's-hair coat who is in treatment because his conscience is tormenting him?

Is this long gray hair really his or is it a dog hair

maybe? On the way home I buy a magnifying glass. Fortunately it looks very much like human hair, with split ends. Monteleone, what a beautiful name. L. for Ludovico? Luigi? Lino? The six days until my next therapy session seem like six years.

The next Wednesday morning I'm up at six. I wash my hair, carefully apply my makeup, put on my best dress. I'm so excited I stop in a bar for a glass of vodka before entering my therapist's waiting room at ten-thirty. I listen to the distant voice; it isn't just sonorous and sympathetic, it's downright sexy. Unfortunately I can't understand what it is he's saying. At one point I think I can make out "Why? Why?" How well I understand him, my Mr. L. Monteleone. Why hasn't the receptionist gone to the restroom for a cigarette today the way she always does? I start to tremble for fear she has given up smoking during the last week, but finally she takes her cigarettes from the drawer, gives me a conspiratorial nod, and disappears. No sooner is she gone than I leap up and fling open the door to the inner office. He isn't lying on the couch, but sitting, just as I do, and that appeals to me right off. His gray hair is almost shoulder length. He and my therapist turn to me in surprise. He is striking, maybe not exactly handsome, but striking is much more interesting than handsome. He looks to be in his early forties, the best age for a man; he's not all that tall, but definitely no shorter than I. "Well, I must say!" my therapist hisses, and I stammer, "Excuse me. I thought it was eleven o'clock already," and close the door, damp with sweat I'm so excited. I scribble a note for the receptionist that I've suddenly taken ill and it's impossible for me to keep my appointment today.

I close the curtains in my apartment. I carefully chisel L. MONTELEONE in the wax; his name is so long it barely fits on the candle. Just as I've been instructed, I rub my body with Come-Hither Oil, light the candle, and hold his hair in the flame. My heart is pounding.

It blazes up faster than eye can see. But the candle burns for four hours and twenty minutes, and for that entire time, so my magic consultants' strict instructions, I have to concentrate on my victim. When the flame finally flickers and goes out, I fall asleep exhausted.

Several hours later the telephone awakens me. In my dream I was in Wuppertal. My mother was crocheting a toilet-paper-holder cover for the car, out of pink wool, and constantly muttering to herself, "There's no pot so dented that a lid won't fit." My answering machine, which I had turned on to keep from being disturbed during the ceremony, answers and explains that I'm not home right now, it beeps, and I hear someone breathing and then a sonorous, sympathetic male voice says, "This is Leonardo Monteleone. What a shame you're not home. . . ."

I leap from the bed, get tangled up in the sheets, can't find the telephone. Leonardo Monteleone, what a name! "What a shame," the voice says, "well, then . . ." I rummage for the cord, follow it clear across the room to the phone. "Wait, wait," I cry out of breath, "I just got in this moment." "My name is Leonardo Monteleone," he repeats politely in almost accent-free English. "You forgot your scarf this morning in the waiting room, a kind of green plaid. . . ."

I never wear green-plaid scarves. "Oh, sure," I say, "that must be mine." Musk rises up from the love sachet under my chin.

"I could bring your scarf over to you."

"That's terribly nice of you. . . ." I stutter.

"Oh," he interrupts, "I didn't mean to be forward. I merely forgot that women in this town don't appreciate total strangers knowing their address."

"You're not from New York?" I ask.

"No, I'm from Germany."

"Oh, really?" I say nonchalantly. "Where then in Germany?"

"Wuppertal, I doubt if that means anything to you."

I take the love sachet from my neck and place it under my pillow.

"I live at 15 Leroy Street," I say slowly and in German. "Come quickly."

"Well, then, tschüss," he says, "see you soon."

I Love You, How
Does That Sound?

"SO WHAT'S the big difference between America and Germany?" Philip thought as he tried to raise the window in his hotel room. The doors open on the wrong side, and you open windows by pushing up. The air rushing into his room was heavy and damp. The police sirens sound different. And the coffee is weaker. He ordered some more. The *y* and *z* are reversed on the typewriters. He had tried with no success to find a typewriter with a German keyboard. I can't, he thought and stretched out on the bed. He didn't miss his wife, and he felt bad about that. The first two weeks without sex were always the worst for him, then he got used to it. Maybe he should have had a cup of coffee with that young musician—she had long, slender legs, and she was part of his article after all, the end of pop music. Legs up to her neck. The longest legs he had ever seen on a woman. He gave her a call.

"The end?" she said. "It's just the beginning. A whole new beginning."

"When you can't even play a chord?"

"That's just it. We can't do a thing and that makes us heavy. So everybody's jealous of us because we can't do anything, and then go ahead and do it anyway."

She was blonde, twenty-five, and said her name was Box. She played with her chopsticks and asked with a giggle if she could have an order of sushi maybe. He drank his fifth sake. She's sweet, he thought.

"The Sex Pistols could play three chords at least," he said.

"That was their big mistake. They had to act as if they were musicians. That's what did them in. We're just hot and can't do a thing."

She bolted down the sushi and hammered away at the table with her chopsticks. He took them away from her. Four little girls in crazy costumes, who were making a pile of money out of nothing. He felt offended.

"You're so European, so damned European," Box said.

He should have just kissed her. She hadn't thanked him for the meal, hadn't even said goodbye. She had just pivoted on the sidewalk and marched off in the opposite direction. Everyone in this city marched, they didn't walk, they ran, head down, toward some imaginary goal. The battle. He watched her white-bleached mop bouncing up and down in the distance. He didn't like New York.

He ordered a beer from room service and tried to write. "We Can't Do a Thing and That Makes Us Heavy." His title depressed him. The waiter arrived with the beer, a stocky young guy who looked Latin American.

"My name is Gabriel Garcia," he said with a thick Spanish accent, "just like the writer."

They smiled at one another; Gabriel crossed his hands behind his back and looked around the room.

"You're a writer, too, right?" He pointed at the typewriter.

"Journalist," Philip said and waited impatiently for the waiter to leave.

"But you think up good stuff, too, right?"

"Well, whatever." Philip poured the beer into a glass. The beer was weaker here, too. Gabriel didn't budge. Philip held the glass out to him.

"I like mine from the bottle anyway."

Gabriel took the glass.

"It's against the rules to join the guests," he said, "but some of them are lonely."

"Do you think I'm lonely?"

"No, no, not you. But the lady up on fifth. She's German, like you. I think she's lonely."

"Aha," Philip said.

"She's really beautiful. I bring her her breakfast every morning. She drinks tea and eats just one egg. She never touches the rest."

"And what makes you think she's lonely?"

Gabriel chugged his beer and smiled.

"How do you say 'I'm crazy about you' in German?" he asked. Philip told him.

"That's hard to say. Could you write it down for me maybe?"

Philip helped Gabriel practice the pronunciation. He had a knack for it. "Ich bin verrückt nach Ihnen. I haven't been able to sleep since the moment I saw you," he read from the piece of paper.

"And this too: if you reject me, I'll be the unhappiest man under the sun."

"That's a lot of German. You can't learn all that by heart," Philip said. "And it may be a little too dramatic . . . for a German lady."

"Oh, no. I'm Puerto Rican, you know. She'll expect it of me."

Gabriel pressed his cheat sheet to his chest and thanked Philip effusively. Once he had gone, Philip felt lonely. He yearned for Box and her long legs. On

TV slender girls in skin-tight leotards were advertising exercise equipment.

He tried to call Box, but there was no answer.

"I'm an old idiot," he thought. He went down to the bar and waited for the German lady from the fifth floor. Three obviously lonely salesmen were sitting at the bar with him. They laughed too loud. "I don't want to end up like them," Philip thought and went back to his room. He couldn't sleep, he was still jet-lagged. He woke up at three o'clock and would have loved to take a walk, but didn't dare risk the streets. He knew they would be able to smell his fear, and that's when things got dangerous. Box would have laughed at him. "What do I want with a twenty-five-year-old chick?" He asked himself. He knew what he wanted from her. What a bore. He took a shower. The shower heads are different in America. Gabriel brought him his breakfast.

"I said it to her last night." He recited the sentences he had learned by heart, and Philip had trouble recognizing them. Gabriel smiled proudly.

The telephone rang. Box was down in the lobby. Philip undressed again and slipped on the robe provided by the hotel. He was having a relaxed breakfast when she arrived.

"I'm sorry," she said. "I thought you'd be up by now."

He offered her coffee. She wanted tea. He ordered tea. Gabriel brought it and gave him a wink.

"Can I take a shower maybe?" Box asked. Philip figured this was a good sign. While she was in the bathroom he made the bed. She came back out again fifteen minutes later, with clothes and makeup on. She drank her tea.

"Are you writing what idiots we are?" she asked.

"No. Of course not."

"What's the title?"

" 'Pop Music Makes a New Beginning,' " he said.

"You see. You did get it."

She was sitting on the couch and pulled her legs up.

"You got a girlfriend?"

"No."

"What's wrong? You split up?"

"Yes," Philip lied.

"Oh, God," Box said, throwing her legs over the sofa arm.

"What do you mean 'oh, God'?"

"Men who've just split up are always trouble, that's what it means."

"Who said I've just split up?"

"I can always feel it."

"Aha."

"I'm learning to play the guitar." She stood up and wandered around the room.

"That's risky, don't you think? 'We can't do a thing and that makes us heavy,' that's your line."

"You never know."

"That's right."

She looked at him. He crossed his legs. His calves were ice cold from the draft of the air-conditioning.

"You never know," she said slowly.

They were silent. She reached for her purse, a tin can with a ribbon attached, pulled out her lipstick.

She bent down over him to look in the mirror as she redrew her lips. He moved to one side. She smelled like baby powder.

She kissed him on the mouth and giggled. He stood up. She waved and let the door fall shut behind her.

He put on socks.

He lay there on the bed all day, listening to the steady noise of traffic. They honk more here than at home, he thought. He didn't search for the switch to the lamp on the nightstand until it was completely dark. The switches are different, little buttons you turn. At ten o'clock Box called. Did he want to have dinner with her?

"I'm very busy," he said. They agreed on the Japanese restaurant.

"That raw fish gives me so much energy," she said.

He arrived too early. He waited for an hour. He

didn't like raw fish. A black mushroom swam in his soup like a stingray. On the way back to the hotel he bought a six-pack of beer. He didn't want to talk with Gabriel Garcia. On TV some sect was advertising its version of salvation, followed immediately by some guy praising guns. Philip remembered something he had once heard: a depressed European closes the window and commits suicide, a depressed American opens the window and shoots everyone in sight.

He pinched his thumb trying to close the window.

He was a ridiculous man. Out of revenge, he called her at eight the next morning. She was so groggy she had to think about who he was. She couldn't remember their having made a date. She wished him a pleasant stay in New York; she was going to the shore to relax for a few days before going on tour.

"You're taking your junk music on tour?" he asked in amazement.

"What do you mean?" Box said cockily. "We're stars."

He hung up and gazed out the window for a while. A black man was dragging a crate behind him, with a doll sitting inside. He stopped, took the doll in his arms, rocked it, put it back in the crate, and slowly shuffled on.

Philip wasn't hungry, but he ordered breakfast.

Gabriel Garcia entered beaming and smiling. He whispered conspiratorially: "I was waiting for you to order breakfast. Guess what, it worked!"

"No," Philip said.

"All night long. A marathon." He made an unambiguous gesture with his hand. "If the management finds out, it means my job. I don't care—I'm the happiest man in the world. I love her. She was so lonely."

Philip had to laugh.

Gabriel Garcia pounded his chest. "I, I made her happy. I can't thank you enough."

He tried to hug Philip, who backed off a couple of steps.

"You really said those sentences I wrote, and it worked?"

"Yes. She loves me now."

"Listen, Gabriel, don't get your hopes too high. That doesn't mean all that much—in Germany."

"She spoke the language of love," Gabriel said with pathos in his voice.

"And she can't speak a word of English?"

"Oh, sure, sure, of course she can."

"Why did I have to write down all that romantic crap in German for you then?"

Gabriel stared at him in surprise.

"She would never have believed me in English. 'I

love you,' how does that sound? Like some pop hit, but not like the truth. I know that. When a woman says 'te quiero' to me, I melt like butter in the sun. But 'I love you,' nobody believes that."

He gave Philip a hearty clap on the shoulder.

"You're a good man. There aren't many like you."

He left. Philip could hear him whistling in the corridor.

He telephoned his wife in Munich.

Girl, You Gotta Love Your Man

THE CAFÉ was empty. They sat down at a wobbly plastic table decorated with a sticky ketchup bottle. CAFÉ OF THE 60S was spelled out backward in the window. Alf laid his head on the table in a patch of sun and closed his eyes. "Careful," Lilli wanted to say, "the table's all sticky too," but held her tongue, didn't want to sound like his mother.

No one came to wait on them. Two kids were killing time behind the counter; one was reading a magazine and constantly pushing his long hair back, the other guy wore a kitchen-towel apron and gaped into the street, never moving.

"I think it's self-service," Lilli said, and when Alf didn't react, "What do you want?"

"Whatever you're having," he muttered without opening his eyes. Lilli had waked up hours before he had, had watched him sleep; he had looked even younger than he was. She stood up and gave the kid with the apron two orders of eggs sunnyside, bacon, coffee, and orange juice. After a long pause he said: "No more fried eggs. It's after twelve."

"But it's on your menu," Lilli replied. The kid with the long hair stared at her blankly, stood up, walked over to the board and rubbed out FRIED EGGS AND BACON. "But we got scrambled," the one with the apron said. Lilli looked straight into his white baby face, so chubby and smooth he looked silly somehow, and said in a stern adult voice, "If you can scramble eggs, you can fry them too." Lilli noticed now that the kid with the long hair was really very cute but just as young as Babyface. He set two Styrofoam cups of coffee in front of her on the counter. "But why can't we have our eggs sunnyside up?" Lilli asked.

"It's like in the sixties," the cute one said. His eyes were fixed on her legs beneath her tiger miniskirt. They still looked quite acceptable; the thighs had some little dimples, true, but you only saw those in the wrong light. "Oh, I see," Lilli said, "like in the sixties . . ." She shook her head and smiled at them both. When they didn't react, just stared impassively at her, Lilli realized it hadn't been meant as a joke. The one with the apron pressed a button on the stereo. Jim Morrison sang "Show me the way to the next whiskey bar."

Alf was singing along as Lilli set his coffee down.

"Do you like scrambled eggs?" she asked him. He shrugged. "Two orders of *scrambled eggs* and bacon," she called to the kids behind the counter. This caused the kid in the apron to yell, "Beate!" A girl with a wild mane of curls, who couldn't have been more than sixteen, came shuffling out of the back room and Babyface pressed a skillet into her hand.

She set the skillet on the stove as if it weighed a ton.

"I tell you we must die," Alf sang. Behind him on the wall was a poster of Jim Morrison, in his famous leather shorts. Lilli had recently read in the paper that they had been auctioned off, and she was sure whoever bought them must have been a woman about her age. "You see, Jim," she thought, "the sexual revolution really did happen. Twelve years later here I am with my lover, who is twelve years younger than me, sitting in a café, and the kids are still listening to your music."

She bent over the table and gave Alf a kiss.

"This is the lousiest coffee I've ever drunk in my whole life," Alf said.

"It's just like in the sixties," Lilli said and laughed.

"What do you mean? Was the coffee that awful back then?" Alf asked, and didn't laugh as he said it. Lilli waited, longing for a laugh, waited and waited, and when it didn't come she suddenly felt as if she were dead drunk and had just walked out of a warm room into icy, crystal-clear air. Of course she had done the addition and subtraction often enough. At twenty-two she would definitely have made quite an impression on ten-year-old Alf, might have been his first big crush, at twelve she could have changed his diapers and fallen in love with a baby, and now at thirty-two she found him more attractive than most men her own age. This kind of math, where twelve never equaled twelve, had amused her, but now, at this very moment, she understood for the first time that she couldn't share a major part of her life with him, and she asked herself what was actually left of it without that part.

"So what?" she thought. "No sentimentality at least."

"Girl, you gotta love your man," Jim Morrison sang now.

"Did you ever see him live?" Alf asked.

"Yes, twice. And I've been to his grave in Paris, too." ◦

"There just aren't any rock stars like that left," Alf said, sighing. "They don't die young anymore. One thing for sure, we had better music back then."

"We?" Lilli thought, but didn't say it.

She watched the girl break four eggs into the skillet, pick up a fork, and stir it around.

"Wait," Lilli shouted and ran over to the counter, "what we really wanted was fried eggs!" The girl looked at her uncomprehendingly. "Just leave them the way they are, that way we get our fried eggs. I really don't like mine scrambled. . . ." The girl took the skillet from the stove and held it out to Lilli. A gooey liquid of half-scrambled eggs slopped around in it. The girl smiled at Lilli and asked shyly, "You want 'em like this?" "No," Lilli said, "go ahead and finish the job." She saw the two kids behind the counter grin. "I know," she said sternly, "it's like in the sixties." The kid with the long hair gave a meaningful nod.

"They're too stupid to fry a couple of eggs sunnyside up," she said softly to Alf as she returned to the table.

"There's a killer on the road," Alf sang.

A group of schoolgirls came drifting into the café. They threw their purses on the chairs and made a dash for the counter. Someone turned the music up. The girls all stared at the door as if expecting someone in particular. They walked back and forth impatiently, danced a few steps, tossed bits of lyrics at one another, flirted for a few bars with the kids behind the counter, then turned back to the door, sucking their Cokes thirstily through straws and tossing their heads back to laugh. One of the girls moved her hips

in rhythm with The Doors. She giggled, rowed with
her arms, went deeper and deeper into her knees,
imitating the twist.

The others were simply convulsed with laughter,
and it slowly dawned on Lilli that these kids apparently believed that back "in the sixties" people had
danced the twist to the Doors. She sought Alf's eyes,
but he was watching the dancing girl's rear end. The
kid with the apron slammed a bell with his hand and
waved to Lilli.

She picked up the two plates of scrambled eggs.
The girl came twisting over her way, went deep into
her knees. Carrying the plates, Lilli balanced past her.
The eggs were unsalted and swimming in grease. Alf
jiggled his knee and gave the girl a nod of encour-
agement. So she turned her rear to him, backing in
closer and wiggling her butt. The other girls tittered.

A man entered the café, about forty, in an elegant
black coat, a Samsonite briefcase in hand. He looked
around, walked resolutely to the counter, and said
something to the kid with the apron. He was handed
coffee in a paper cup. He set his briefcase down, took
a few cautious sips from the cup, and checked out
the girls. He gave a little shake of his head, then his
eyes fell on Lilli. They looked at each other. He lifted
his cup of coffee as if to toast her. Lilli nodded, stretch-
ing her arm across the table for Alf's hand. He looked

up in surprise. "I tell you, we must die," Jim Morrison sang. The man picked up his Samsonite briefcase. As he left he brushed his arm across Lilli's back.

"Excuse me," Lilli said to Alf.

The man was loading the briefcase into his Mercedes. Lilli was standing face to face with him now, breathless. The man eyed her coolly.

"Let me tell you one thing right off," he said, "I hate sentimentality."

Financial Times

IT'S JUST an in-between job, understand? You don't even have to be all that young or especially pretty. Some are forty and over. The agency requires you to be attractive in some way and well educated, otherwise they won't take you. I told them I had a master's in art history, which isn't true of course, but I did study four semesters. It's enough if you read the newspaper, you're sure to find something to talk about. Most of them think it's quite charming, too, if you're not all that knowledgeable. They want to relax, you know. I don't negotiate the deal, that's the agency's job. They take the calls from the hotels, only the best ones; they don't give out the phone number to the others. I bought myself an answering machine, too, because who would pass up a cool thousand for a couple of hours of work? Usually I just go out to dinner with them, they're generally way too tired for anything else. But even if that's what they do want, I can always turn them down; the agency is fair, they don't force it. Yesterday evening I had intended to go see the Pretenders, I'm crazy about their music, but then the agency called. They give you just a first name and a time: Daniel, 8 p.m., Hotel Kurfürst. I liked his name right off; they're usually named Peter or Fritz. Men with so much power must be something special, that's what you think when you start; most of them have good manners, but not much more than that. They're ugly, too, most of them. I can spot them on the street now. They always wear the same shoes, custom-made and the toes have all these little holes, brown or black. They have bad skin, smoke a lot. The young ones don't have potbellies, because that's not dynamic, but the older ones almost always do; they have so much power that they don't have to worry about it anymore. Their suits always shimmer just the least bit, that's how you can tell it's expensive fabric. They all eat much too fast, because they are used to not having enough time. And there's usually a boarding-pass stub in the suit jacket.

So I took a nice long bath and put on a beauty mask. Sometimes I'm really not in the mood, but I convince myself I've got a date with the man of my dreams; if your heart's not in it it's pure torture. I put on my emerald dress; it looks especially good on me, picks up the color of my eyes. The wardrobe is an investment, of course. I borrowed the money from my mother, told her I needed books for my courses. I don't ever want to get old and have varicose veins like my mother. They wind clear up her legs, she's got weak tissue, I've inherited it from her. Sometimes I can already see the dark shadows of the veins on my legs, and I'm only twenty-six. I'll quit at twenty-eight at the latest and take a sensible job. Haven't the vaguest what it'll be. Right now I'm a social worker, providing businessmen with a pleasant evening, that's how I see it.

The desk clerk nodded, he knows me, and the men in the lounge turned around to get a look at me. When I want to, I can look first class.

I sat down on a couch and paged through the *Financial Times*. I like the pink paper. I memorized headlines; it's usually enough if you can quote headlines, then they take over all on their own. Talk about "Coca-Cola to Leave South Africa," for example; a headline like that is money in the bank. They all have something to say about it, whether they're politicians or businessmen.

"Miss Carla?" he asked. That isn't my real name of course. We call our customers by their first names, but use formal pronouns, that's how the agency wants it. I let him ask twice before I lowered my newspaper.

They have to go to a little trouble; that makes them feel better afterward and forget they've hired you. He wasn't particularly tall or especially good-looking for a man with power. His hair was cut medium long and flecked with gray, like his beard. I like it when these men wear their hair a little longer, it adds a brash touch. The brash touch went as far as his belt, because he had pulled his pants up so high they almost reached his armpits, made him look awfully stuffy; my father's the only other man I know who wears his pants like that. We shook hands, we walked through the lobby, he put his arm around my shoulder. They all do that, want to make it look as if we've known each other for a while; somebody they work with may be watching.

Let me tell you, there's nothing more boring than a steady diet of fine dining. There's always something with salmon, and the sauces are always so rich your stomach feels queasy. They use alcohol in everything, and those affected waiters get on my nerves. So we had taken our seats in this three-star restaurant—the waiters always shove the chair in under your behind as if you were too stupid to manage it by yourself—and so we were sitting there, studying the menu, and Daniel said what he really felt like was spinach, fried eggs, and potatoes. I liked him right off. Only men like him can pull off leaving a restaurant like that; that's how you can tell they have class.

I figured him for a politician, but he was the boss of a big clock concern; you'd recognize the name, I'm sure, but the secret of my job is discretion. He was in town to offer a TV anchorman a contract to wear one of their watches. That wasn't allowed, of course, but they all did it, he said. "You can't imagine what all a TV audience sees. They're aware of every detail." He had once been friends with a woman who answered the mail for a TV network. She had told him all the things the audience notices, and how they write that they hadn't liked the anchor's tie on the seven-o'clock news on Tuesday, how the guy on the other channel was wearing a much more tasteful one. We both laughed; he looked very young despite the gray in his hair. I guessed mid-forties. He ate his fried eggs with just his fork, had the best of manners. We talked about movies; I know something about that, turn on my TV early every morning. I just like to have the picture going, that way I'm not so alone in my room. Did I like being alone, he asked. Who did, I said. There was a difference, he said, between lonely and alone, you always hoped you'd make it to the top, and then when you got there the air was so thin and you were so terribly lonely. They all say that, I've heard it before. I really can't imagine it, but I always smile sympathetically and sometimes I take their hands. But not his, he wasn't the type for that. "The dangerous thing about power," he said, "the dangerous thing is that you no longer have to take the usual detours to get what you want. Neither on the job nor in your personal life. One call suffices. You get what you want. It's very practical, and it's a lot of fun at the start. You feel truly powerful. And you realize you're getting everything you want, but there's no emotional investment, do you understand what I mean?" It's dangerous to answer questions like that, because, whatever you say, they feel you don't understand. So I said nothing, just looked at him. They usually go right on talking. He did too. "I can remember not getting that first big advertising contract for the little company I was working for, how I sat there on the bed in my hotel room, more a rundown pension than a hotel, and bawled. It was all over for me at that moment; I wanted to pack my bags and just drop out. No matter what I do nowadays, I try never to forget how I felt that day, because otherwise I'd be haunted by the feeling that life was better then."

I liked him because he had bawled that day. Sometimes they tell you stories like that to get you into bed. Not him. "Thanks for listening," he said. It had been a lovely evening, and riding back with him in the taxi to his hotel, I made up my mind that I would go on home. He squeezed my hand and got out. I waved. Then he opened the door again and asked if I might be interested in joining him at the bar for a drink. I knew the bar had already closed.

He had a suite; you can always rank them according to that. Sometimes they tell you how in reality they're the ones who run the country, and then all they have is a single. I prefer the ones who play down their power. So he had a suite. To start with he sat opposite me and we talked about period furniture. I don't know why I made such a thing of it. I was more taken by him than by most of them, than by any of them ever before, maybe that's why. When he sat down beside me on the couch I should either have left right then or said yes. Instead I said I couldn't do it, not for just one night. He wasn't surprised, which surprised me. He said something very strange, he said, "Every long relationship begins with just one night." And my reaction was to turn very shy. He tried to kiss me, and I squirmed for a long time like a little girl. I simply liked him too much, understand? When I feel shy I act very cool. "A long relationship?" I said ironically. "Let's forget the sweet talk. You hired me, and I've belonged to you, that's all." "Yes?" he said, a soft, long-drawn-out yes. I couldn't simply leave. He was one of the good kissers, and there aren't many of them; most men don't know how to kiss at all. "It's not going to happen," I said. "That's okay," he said, "I just want to kiss you."

It was four in the morning before I undressed. He laid out his clothes very carefully, then picked up my high heels and set one beside the other.

I like men with a little meat on their bones, like him, and a little out of shape. I find it touching. I tend to be put off by young, tight musclemen. I like it to be a little sad, the flesh I mean, not so natural somehow. He called me his sweetheart, and normally I wouldn't have reacted to that sort of crap at all. But at that moment I really was his sweetheart. His face above me suddenly looked much older, because the skin sort of droops then; I wonder if mine is like that already, too.

I told him how much fun it is when men with power suddenly become soft and helpless like little babies. I possess them for a little while, and no one can take that away from me again. He lay on my breast and muttered something I didn't understand, then he fell asleep. That would really have been the ideal moment to get up very quietly and disappear. I went into the bathroom and smoked a cigarette. I looked through his toilet kit. You learn more about a man from that than from his passport. He had tiny scissors and a brush in a little case, probably for his beard. And moisturizing cream, a very expensive brand. Vitamin pills. They always have those. And a rinse to bring out the silver in his gray hair. I don't find that unmanly at all; I like for men to be vain. So he uses a rinse on his hair. Sweetheart. I lay down, snuggling very close to him and imagining we were married. Just so, for the fun of it. The wake-up call came at six. He held me tight in his embrace. It was slower than the first time, more emotion in it. The telephone rang right in the middle. He stayed beside me while he took the call. It was about money. He gave some brief instructions; it sounded very cool and businesslike. I sat there smiling. They know how to do that, these men with power, doesn't matter what the situation, they always can sound alert, cool, and businesslike.

The call lasted too long. After that it just didn't work. He apologized.

I was afraid of the moment when he would suddenly be in a hurry, hardly look at me, and speak to me in that same cool, businesslike tone. I was sure it would happen; there's a good reason why they all have made it to the top. At some point they start to function like machines; some of them take longer to shift into gear, but they all do it. Not him.

We ate breakfast together like an old married couple, he in his bathrobe and I in my panties and bra. That was the loveliest part, maybe. We didn't say much; at one point he put my legs on his lap and rubbed them. Then he said, "You're something very special." Ah yes.

He gave me his watch. I'm lying on my bed, curtains closed. I stare at the dial on his watch and feel how we are growing older together.

No Baggage

I WAS GLAD to have got a compartment all to myself. First I pulled the curtains to discourage anyone else from entering. When the train finally started moving, I was still alone. I pulled off my shoes and stretched out. I wanted to sleep all eight hours to Hamburg. I was going to call my parents from the airport and tell them I had missed my connecting flight to Hanover and would be spending the night in Munich. But I didn't have any German change on me, and so they would be at the Hanover airport now, waiting for their son, who wouldn't arrive. I hadn't the least desire to see them again, not even after two years in America. The first German I wanted to see was Marita in Hamburg. She wasn't so unbearably German, or at least hadn't been back then. Two years had taught me how to react like an American. When the captain of our Lufthansa flight came on the loudspeaker, it made me think of the Nazi bastards on American TV and not much else.

No, I hadn't wanted to come back.

In Augsburg a woman flung the compartment door open and sat down without a word. She didn't ask if there was a vacant seat or even say "Good morning." I sullenly turned over on the other side but couldn't fall back asleep. I felt as if I were being watched. I sat up. She was in her early thirties maybe, plump, with a quite pretty, clear face. Her eyes were slightly swollen. She wore long silver earrings that swayed lightly to the rhythm of the train. I didn't see any baggage and that was a relief. She couldn't be going far. She held her purse clamped tight as if she were afraid I was going to snatch it. Our eyes met by chance, and she quickly looked away. I saw little beads of sweat on her forehead.

"Can I open the window a little?" she asked in a soft but definite voice.

If I answer her now she's going to tell me the story of her life, I thought. "I'm sorry, I don't speak German."

She repeated her question. "Ze vindow. Can I open?"

I nodded. She put her head out the window. Her

hair fluttered. I felt chilly. I pulled on my jacket. She closed the window and sat back down.

I was about to pull out my newspapers, when I remembered the only ones I had were German. I got up to see if I could find another empty compartment. But even all the ones in first class were occupied. When I came back she was dabbing at her eyes with a handkerchief. The sun set.

A man in an orange jacket passed by, pushing a cart and selling sandwiches and beverages.

"One coffee, white, and a salami sandwich," I told him. He looked at me uncomprehendingly. "Einen Kaffee und ein Salamibrot," she translated for me. "What he means by 'white' I don't know."

"With milk," I said. She threw me a quick smile. But afterward I wasn't certain whether she had smiled at all, it was over so quickly, as if she had pulled a curtain shut. She stared blankly out the window. I turned on the compartment light. "Zis is better," she said, turning it off again and clicking on the little reading lamp above my head. She sat in the dark. I could barely make out her face.

"You are from America?"

"Yes."

"Where?"

"New York."

"It's a dangerous city, no?"

I could have kicked myself for claiming I didn't speak German. Now she was going to tell me her life story anyway, only in ghastly English.

"I speak a little German," I said with a thick American accent.

"But you said before that . . ."

"I'm a little shy. Long time no speaked."

"But you really speak quite well. Where did you learn?"

"My parents are German."

She fell silent. I prayed she had nothing more to say.

"Emigrants?" she asked. I didn't answer to keep from getting involved any further.

"My grandfather died in a concentration camp," she said. "He was a Communist."

The train stopped. She didn't get out. How could anyone travel over 250 miles without any baggage? And a woman at that? Her purse was tiny; you couldn't fit so much as a cosmetic bag in it.

"I was very lucky with my parents, you know? It was pure accident that they weren't Nazis . . . I've always asked myself what that must be like, to leave everything behind, from one day to the next, and not know if you're ever coming back."

"Just be glad that's not how it is these days," I said,

and my artificial American accent was getting on my nerves. It sounded so flippant, ignorant, and stupid.

"But it could get that way again."

"You think so?"

"I don't know."

Suddenly she was sitting beside me with her head leaning on my shoulder. I liked her. I liked her because of what she had said. She was not a typical German. I didn't move. She sighed, and I saw a teardrop on the red plastic between us. I put my arm around her.

"Why are you crying?"

"I'd rather not talk about it," she said and laid her hand on my knee. I took hold of it, held it tight. People might have taken us for a pair of lovers.

"Are you vacationing in Germany?" she asked, trying to make small talk.

I don't like to talk about myself. But I told her everything. Maybe because she had been crying. In broken German I told her the whole stupid story of my American love affair. After a while I began to like it, pronouncing the words wrong, asking her for the right word, stammering.

I was forced to unfold my tale of woe in a vocabulary of two hundred words, and the longer I spoke the clearer the whole story became to me. There hadn't been any hope with Cathy from the very beginning.

"And you've left your country because of a woman?"

"Yes," I said, "just because of a woman. Breaked heart."

She kissed me. I switched off the reading lamp.

She pulled the seats out, turning the compartment into a giant bed. We held each other, embraced and kissed.

When I woke up I thought for a moment it was Cathy lying beside me. She brushed her hand across my eyes.

"Don't cry," she said. "There are worse things."

She was about to roll up the blind.

"Don't," I said.

"We'll soon be there."

"I want to stay just like this. Never get off," I said.

"That's not possible." She laughed for the first time all night. We were in Hamburg.

She pushed the seats back and rolled up the blind. She was holding her purse clamped tight, she gazed at me.

"Why don't you have any baggage?" I asked softly. She looked at the floor, then raised her head and looked me straight in the eye.

"I've just stepped out to get some cigarettes," she said.

I acted as if I didn't understand the phrase.

"I have three kids and a husband. Yesterday evening I left the house . . . just left." She looked surprised.

We walked together along the platform. I wanted to tell her everything. That I wasn't an American at all, that my parents weren't emigrants, that I could speak German. That the story about Cathy was a true story.

When I turned around she had vanished. I waited a half hour. Then I called Marita. She wasn't home.

I looked in my bag for a cigarette. I found a long silver earring.

What Do You Want from Me?

"SCHWITTER, KUBECK, and Reimer, good morning. Yes, he's in. But his line is busy right now. Can you hold? Schwitter, Kubeck, and Reimer, good morning," it goes on like that from nine in the morning until five or five-thirty every evening. I have a telephone voice, a lot of people have told me that. For lunch I bring some cereal from home. The firm appreciates the fact that I stay at the phone; it leaves a bad impression if there is no answer at lunchtime. Two years ago they got me a headset with a mike fitted right at my mouth, but I still have the pains in my neck. Ten out of a hundred callers at most say thank you. When I call a company or a government office, I'm especially friendly to the operator. The music sets the tone, I always say, and I'm the first impression anyone has of our firm. The first impression is crucial.

While I take calls, I try to read a good book. I

seldom manage more than five pages a day. I read only three today, because all hell broke loose. There are days when everybody and his brother calls here, and other days when the phone rings once every fifteen minutes.

The doctor told me I should walk a lot, for my neck pain, and so as soon as I get home at night I change into comfortable shoes and take a walk until the eight-o'clock news.

I walk past the gas station that's closed down. There's lilac blooming there now, once it's dark I may cut off a branch or two. Nobody should get upset about that, the lilac doesn't really belong to anyone since the gas station went out of business. There's a new weight-loss supplement in the window of my corner drugstore; it's called MPL, M for maple syrup, P for pollen, and L for lemon. I hardly eat anything anymore and I still gain weight. All I want is to be able to look in the big closet mirror sometime and be content with what I see. I only do it for myself. I don't see anyone all day anyway, so in that sense it doesn't make any difference what I look like, but it does to me. I always dress properly for work; I don't like people who let themselves go just because nobody is going to see them.

I always set the table for dinner; I never eat cold cuts from the wrapping paper or drink milk out of the carton. The delicatessen on Hohenzollern Strasse has marvelous salads with no preservatives added, but I've been denying myself of late; there's cream in them, and that puts on the weight.

When the stores close at six-thirty, the streets are suddenly as good as dead. I walk the length of Hohenzollern Strasse, but never out onto Leopold Strasse; in summer it's as good as a tenderloin. Oh, most of them act as if they're just having coffee in the sidewalk cafés, but their eyes latch onto every man under thirty who happens to stroll by, I call it the meat rack. I didn't like it when I was still in my twenties either, and that wasn't all that long ago.

Before I get to Leopold Strasse, I turn left down Wilhelm Strasse, and then walk as far as Clemens Strasse. I've got into the habit of walking the same route; I find it soothing to keep track of the tiniest changes and still notice how most things stay the same.

I've seen this tall man with the thick black hair several times before in the neighborhood. He's always alone, just walking around. Sometimes he stands on a corner lost in thought, hands behind his back, watching the traffic. Must be about my age, not really good-looking, but there's something attractive about him. That's as far as my interest goes. Even if it doesn't sound quite like that maybe, he interests me as much or as little as a pair of new shoes in that sinfully expensive shop just off Hohenzollern Strasse.

He is walking in the same direction as I am, but he's dawdling, and it's not long before I pass him. The doctor said I should keep up a good, steady pace, otherwise there's no point. I can feel him behind me; he's wearing a light gray jacket today, usually it's blue. He walks more slowly than I do, but his strides are longer, and soon he is beside me again. He glances my way, and I start walking faster.

There is more traffic on Clemens Strasse, so I can't hear his steps now. I don't want to look around, but I'm sure he turned off a good while ago. I stop at a shop window and suddenly spot him in the reflection. He is standing right behind me!

Up till now it might have been purely accidental. Maybe it still is. Maybe he's really interested in the gift-shop knickknacks, overpriced and foolish stuff. Without turning around, I move away and walk on. My heart is pounding noticeably, how annoying. How silly. It's still broad daylight, a man goes for a walk in Schwabing, and happens to stop in front of the same shop I do. But I can hear his steps again. I walk faster and depart from my usual route. Maybe I can shake him off. I start to run, run back to Hohenzollern Strasse. I start to get a stitch in my side, that always happens very quickly, it always got me excused from gym class in school. When you reach a certain age, you stop running, you no longer make a fool of yourself by running after buses, you wait for the next one instead. I feel like I'm making a fool of myself now, rushing along Friederich Strasse holding my side. The blood is pounding in my ears. I can't hear him now, I stop, he's gone. I lean against a wall, gasping, and the pain in my side slowly lets up. I can only shake my head at myself. Maybe the problem is that I'm alone too much. You start imagining things, you start talking to yourself, and it's easy just to let yourself go if you don't watch out. "Anne, you hysterical, stupid old lady," I say to myself and walk on.

First I see his shadow. He's standing in front of me, smiling. The sound that comes out is really very odd, when all I want to say is: "Leave me alone! Go away! What do think you're doing?" But all that comes out of my mouth is this strange sound, and he smiles. I decide not to run, but to walk at a firm, steady pace. He follows me. I walk past the delicatessen again, past the drugstore, the gas station that's out of business, I try to think of something else, but the clack, clack, clack of his steps behind me makes that impossible. A taxi drives by, I could have hailed it, too late. The one thing I should not do is go home, but where can I go, where can I hide until he disappears? Not that he looks like a madman, he looks more pleasant than most in fact. I want to go home, just get home, close the door behind me and turn on the TV, then it will all be over.

I can't find the right key, he's standing behind me. Usually I can unlock the door in total darkness. Finally I'm in the entry, I push the heavy door shut, the bolt snaps, I don't wait for the elevator, I run up the three flights and start coughing I'm so out of breath. I slide the chain into place and double-lock the door.

My favorite show is on TV, but I can't really concentrate on it. Usually I guess along with the contestants, and if I win I reward myself with a piece of chocolate or a cognac, sometimes even two.

I tiptoe to my door and look through the peephole. The hallway is dark—and empty. I could have sworn ... I open the door just to be on the safe side. His foot is in the door faster than I can see it happen. I'm terrified, but can't make a sound. He shuts the door from inside.

"What do you want?" I ask softly, very softly. He rocks his head, smiles that strange smile of his, goes to the kitchen, opens the fridge, takes out the butter and cold cuts as if he knows exactly where they are. He sits down at my kitchen table and makes himself a sandwich.

"Please! What do you want from me?" I'm holding tight to the door frame. I could run to the neighbors, but they wouldn't even lend me a couple of eggs when I was baking a cake one Sunday. Didn't have any. Neither neighbor had any eggs. Likely story. They don't like me because I told them not to park their baby carriages right in front of my door.

"I'm going to call the police," I say in a firm, very firm voice. He looks at me. There's something attractive about his face. He's eating now, then he's going to kill me, and rob the house. I lock myself in the living room and call the police. When I come back to the kitchen he has drunk all my milk. I can't drink my morning coffee without real milk. Now I'll have to go get milk tomorrow morning, which means I'll have to get up ten minutes early. You think of the most ordinary things in the most extraordinary situations.

"I've called the police. They'll be here any minute."

Maybe he doesn't believe me. He doesn't budge. His fingernails are clean, he eats his open-face sandwich with a knife and fork. He'll stab me with the fork. A ridiculous death for a ridiculous woman. I surreptitiously check the clock. I called the police four minutes ago. He doesn't seem all that dangerous.

"What do you want from me?" I ask him for the third time. No answer. I pull a chair over to the kitchen door. We wait.

The two policemen eye me suspiciously. They are

hardly more than twenty. Rookies. I lead them into the kitchen, point at him. He has folded his hands on the table and he smiles. Then a deep, melodic voice says, "Ms. Schwarz"—that is my name—"Ms. Schwarz is a relative of mine, and we've had a little argument about an inheritance an uncle left us." He says it very calmly and never stops smiling. I start to stammer, and as an operator I know how stupid and unbelievable that sounds. I can always tell from that whether someone really has an appointment or is just faking. "I . . . I don't know this man at all," I stammer and immediately I've lost the two young cops with my stammering.

"He followed me. I went for a walk, and he followed me," I say now a little more clearly, and he nods. "That's true, I did follow Ms. Schwarz, because she kept hanging up on me whenever I called, and wouldn't have answered her door in any case." "He stuck his foot in the door and forced his way in. I swear to you I've never seen this man before." That was a lie. I never lie, really, but the fact that I've noticed him several times before on my walks has nothing to do with this. "My cousin, she's my cousin, twice removed, and wants nothing to do with me," he says. The two policemen make a routine check of his ID. They shift their weight from leg to leg, and one of them says, "You'll have to straighten out your family problems among yourselves." At the door I beg them to believe me, one just shrugs and the other says, "If your cousin gets violent, give us a call."

"He's not my cousin!" I shout after them.

He is sitting watching TV, the news.

"You were very clever with the police. But now you're going to leave. I'm begging you, leave!" I stand in front of the TV to block his view. He twists his head around so as not to miss anything. Then he stands up, pulls the other armchair over beside him, nods to me, and sits back down.

I pour myself a cognac and give him one, too. "Thanks," he says. That is the first word he has said to me. We watch TV together. He has long, slender hands, they lie on long, slender legs. Sometimes he laughs at something on TV. I pour us both a second cognac.

"You've fixed this place up nice," he says. I smile. I went to a lot of trouble decorating it. All the colors match, I had the walls papered in a pale salmon, the chairs are beige, the curtains dark red. I enjoy coming home to my pretty little apartment every evening. I hand him the remote for the TV.

"Pick out what you want," I say. I don't care what we watch.

He switches to a detective story. I don't like to watch detective stories this late; I can't get to sleep then. When I'm alone. Bang! go the guns, tires squeal. "What do you want from me?" I say very softly amid a hail of bullets. He doesn't hear me. He pulls his chair closer to mine, and takes my hand when I flinch at someone holding a knife to the throat of a beautiful young blonde.

He doesn't let go until the station goes off the air and snow is drifting across the screen. We just sit there and stare into the snow.

"I'll buy some hard rolls in the morning," he says, "and milk for your coffee."

Tomorrow is Friday. I'm off at four on Fridays. I don't like weekends at all. Even less happens then than usual. I get up, turn off the TV. It is so still, so terribly still. I could go for one more turn around the block, maybe he'll be there again, on the corner of Wilhelm Strasse and Clemens Strasse. There is something attractive about his face.

I could go by the gas station and pick some lilacs. No one gives me flowers anymore, that's for sure. I often buy some for the weekend. I put them on the round table in the living room, sniff at them now and then, and some man I don't know has sent them to me.

With Knife and Fork

MY MOTHER claims she should have seen it coming. I had been that way even as a little girl—never satisfied, spiteful. She visits twice a month and brings me Nescafé, cigarettes, magazines, sometimes a lipstick, some green eye shadow today, it's the latest thing on the outside, she says and bites into an apple.

I can't help it. My mother makes such funny noises when she eats an apple. It makes chills run up my spine, I start to tremble and just want to murder her.

It's always been that way. I used to be able simply to leave the room. She called me cold and heartless for getting up and leaving while she poured out her woes about my father, but should I have told her that the way she eats an apple turns my stomach? She can't help it.

My father always rubbed one foot against the other. When he would sit there in his slippers watching TV, no matter how hard I tried all I could hear was the constant scuffing noise of his slippers. Drove me simply crazy, sometimes I had to hold my ears to keep from screaming at him.

So it all started very early on. I thought it would stop at some point, would stop if I could find one person I truly liked, with all his shortcomings. My parents drove me crazy, but that's perfectly normal, isn't it?

I fell in love for the first time at age sixteen. He was eighteen and had very big brown eyes. He wore his hair long, such fine baby hair, I always brushed it for him. I would have done anything for him. When he was drafted and stationed up in the moors, I ran away from home and got a room in Lüneburg just to be near him. I worked in a bakery to pay the rent. The smell of fresh bread clung to my clothes and hair, no matter how often I showered, I couldn't get rid of it, and couldn't eat bread anymore either.

He was very sweet to me. On our first anniversary he gave me a really expensive pair of earrings. I ought to have felt satisfied.

But then he lost his hair. Even though he was only nineteen. It got thinner and thinner, and then it got oily. It started to remind me of leftover spaghetti. I washed it for him every day, but it stayed oily all the same. I couldn't run my hand through his hair without having to go wash my hands right away. But I did it secretly, I didn't want to hurt him. I talked him into a crew cut by cutting out magazine pictures of men with real short hair and showing them to him, until he finally went to the barber. That helped, too, but only for a short time, until he was discharged, and then he swore he would never wear his hair short again because it reminded him of the army. The day he proposed to me his hair was hanging in oily strands down to his collar. Maybe he should have asked me early in the morning. When his hair was freshly washed it wasn't so bad. He was really a sweet guy.

After that it was a long time before I found a man I really liked. By the second or third date I knew that at some point I would come to hate him for the slobbery way he talked, for the way he twirled his mustache, for his habit of buttoning the top button on his shirt, or for constantly hitching up his pants.

I'm critical, that's all. Of myself, too. I'm no beauty, my legs are too short, so I never wear short skirts, my mouth is lopsided, so I apply my lipstick to make it less noticeable, my face is a little too round, which means I would never have my hair cut short. As far as I know, I don't have any unpleasant habits. And when I do discover one—tugging my ear when I'm unsure of myself for instance—I try to correct it. I am never going to get fat. A single pound too many on my ribs, and I feel sick, and don't feel better until

I've starved it off. Doesn't every woman want to be beautiful?

I don't like handsome men. I'm suspicious of them, because they think they can have it all just because they were born with pretty faces. They really can't help it.

It was different with Berthold. He didn't even know that he was handsome. I waited a long time for the moment when something about him would bother me. I was very careful. When I still found him flawless after six months, we got married. I couldn't get enough of looking at him. I watched him every morning while he washed and shaved. I liked everything, absolutely everything about him. He could eat apples without making a sound, never once did I catch him with oily hair, he always looked elegant—he was attractive even when he had the sniffles. He was so attractive that I went to a lot of trouble keeping pace with him. I've never felt so beautiful as I did with him. Back then I wouldn't even have objected to children, although I sometimes asked myself whether I could have loved them the way you're supposed to love your children. You can't pick and choose in that case. But I had picked my Berthold.

And it never would have happened if he hadn't been promoted and suddenly had such a long lunchtime that he could come home to eat. We had always had breakfast together, of course, and in the evening our cold cuts and cheese. And we never ate a big dinner on Sunday. During the week I would fix myself a warm meal now and then, but never for him, since he never came home until evening and never wanted a warm meal because he kept a close eye on his waistline. He didn't like to go out to eat, either—he was always having business lunches in restaurants. But now he was coming home every noon. I noticed it right away. He shoved the whole meal into a mound in the center of his plate and stirred till it was slop. I could feel myself suddenly turn cold, ice-cold, even though it was summer and we were eating out on the terrace. Each time he stuck his fork into the slop it made a smacking sound, and then another, and another. He asked me if I wasn't hungry at all, and I quickly stood up and ran to the bathroom. I wasn't sick at my stomach. I was afraid.

I had to turn my head away as I carried his leftover slop to the kitchen, but that didn't help. He was lying on the sofa taking a short noon nap. I wanted to lie down next to him and doze off with him for a few minutes, forget the whole thing, but I couldn't. I could picture every detail: him shoveling each forkful of slop into his mouth, swallowing, the slop lying there in his stomach, fermenting. I shuddered in disgust. From then on I made soups, until he complained. I was able to justify the steaks and salad by telling him I simply had to take off some weight and didn't think it would matter to him if he supported me in the effort. I was trying to save my marriage. After three weeks he didn't want to see another salad, he wasn't a rabbit, he said, and I was thin enough already, overdoing it in fact. He said he wanted Swedish meatballs and mashed potatoes, and the mere thought brought tears to my eyes. He started criticizing me. All I could think about, he said, was my figure, so from here on out he was going to cook his own midday meal.

When he took over the kitchen at noon, I went to the bedroom until he was done with his meal. A couple of times he begged me at least to provide him some company. I tried it once. Peas, potatoes, hamburger steak, straight from the can to his plate. When he picked up his fork and stirred it all up, I tried to look in some other direction. But I could hear the sound.

From then on, everything about him bothered me. He was just like the way he ate. He had always been a hazy thinker, never ending his sentences, and now I could see how all his thoughts got stirred into slop in his brain, how he stuck his fork in it and then tried to feed it to me. I couldn't listen to him anymore, I couldn't stand him anymore.

I would leave the house at noon, flee to my bed

before he came home in the evening, get up in the morning only after he had already left for work. He pleaded with me to tell him what was wrong.

Once I dreamed I was lying next to him in bed and suddenly I felt something warm and wet on my skin, and when I turned over I saw his belly had burst open and a thick, yellow-green slop was oozing out of him, more and more of it, until it ran down off the covers onto the floor, filling up the room, spilling out the windows, rising higher and higher, and I was going to drown in it. I screamed in terror. When I woke up he was holding me in his arms. His touch was worse than the dream. From then on we slept in separate beds. I don't know which of us was unhappier.

One day he came home early, and I was standing in the kitchen brewing a cup of tea. He closed the door and said we had to talk. We couldn't go on living like this. He started to thaw a package of frozen spinach. Broke two eggs into the skillet. It looked as if I were trying to run from him, he said. He poured hot milk into the instant potatoes. I tried to look out the window and think of something else. He took my arm and forced me to sit down. He didn't touch his food, not for a good while.

He spoke about love. I really did try. I tried with

all my might. I told him that I loved him, too, really. He said nothing and looked at me for a long time. Then he picked up his fork. Mashed potatoes, spinach, and fried eggs. I don't remember the rest. In court, they showed me a long knife in a plastic bag.

Why Are You
Calling Me?

ACTUALLY I never answer the phone, because it could be my mother wanting to know how things are going with Albert and me. Badly. And she knows that perfectly well.

"Hello," he said. "Am I speaking with Carla Breszinski?"

"Yes, what can I do for you?"

"I don't really know."

"Where did you get my number?"

"From the telephone book."

Then he was silent. I couldn't tell his age; he had a deep voice.

"Who are you? And why are you calling me?"

"You're doing okay, I hope."

"Tell me why you're calling, please. Otherwise I'll hang up."

He was silent. I don't know why I didn't hang up right then.

"How are *you* doing?" I asked.

"That's the point."

"Listen . . ."

"I'm listening."

"You're not doing too well, I take it."

"I didn't say that."

"I'm going to hang up now."

"Sorry I disturbed you. And take care of yourself."

He hung up. I started to cook. I don't like to cook, but Albert likes me to. He never talks to me, but he's happy to eat my cooking. He can't decide. I asked him if he even loves me. He doesn't know. He needs time; I should just leave him alone.

I almost didn't hear the phone; I always have the radio on when I'm cooking.

"Hello," he said.

I waited.

"Does this weather make you feel tired, too?"

"It's not so bad."

"My name's August Tammik, in case you're interested."

"August? Is that a joke?"

"No."

"What do you want from me?"

"Nothing."

"Why are you calling me then? Did you just pick

a name at random from the book? Do we know each other from somewhere?"

"No."

"Well, all the best. Goodbye."

I just sat there for a while. Then I noticed the corner of the rug was pulled back. I stood up to straighten it and the telephone rang again.

"Yes?" I said.

"What's wrong? You sound so strange."

"I do? When are you coming over?"

"I'm not coming over this evening," Albert said.

"You have a date with her?"

He hung up. I flushed the food down the toilet. There was nothing on TV. I went to bed early. It rang for a good while before it woke me up.

"Hello," he said. "Did I wake you up?"

"No. I'm glad you called."

"Can we meet somewhere? Right now?"

"I'm already in bed."

"It's important."

"Why do you want to see me? We don't even know each other."

He gave me the address of a bar. It was empty. I ordered a vodka tonic and sat down at a table. They covered their tablecloths with glass. That's practical, I thought.

He was short, about my age, around thirty. He

seemed nervous. First he went to the john, then to the jukebox, sat down, ran both hands through his hair.

"I just said goodbye to the woman I wanted to marry," he said and grinned.

"And that was what you wanted to talk to me about?"

"She's getting married in the morning. All we did was fight. I just got her wedding announcement yesterday."

He had a little gap between his front teeth. I liked it.

"I went to see her today and asked her if she didn't really want to marry me. She turned me down."

"I see," I said lamely.

"I don't particularly like her." He grinned again.

"Did you notice the fish?"

There were large plastic fish on the walls, sharks and carp.

"I've got a big fish like that, too. She gave me one."

He laid his hand on mine. I let him keep it there. He didn't move it. I drank another vodka tonic. He stared at me. I wanted to see the gap in his teeth.

"Are you sad that you've lost her for good?"

"What?" He smiled in surprise, and there it was again, the gap in his teeth. "I was just making up a story."

"Oh, I see. Why did you call me then, really?"

"And here we are together."

"I have to go." I was reaching for my coat, and he took hold of my hand.

"Are you as hungry as I am?" he asked.

The restaurants had closed by then. We went to a fast-food place. He put his arm around my shoulder. He was almost a head shorter than I.

"What are you laughing at?"

"You're so much shorter than I am. That feels strange."

He took his arm from my shoulder.

"See that waiter there? He's actually an actor, knows all of Shakespeare by heart, but he doesn't like for you to talk about it."

The waiter shoved our hamburgers across the counter. He had greasy black hair and torn fingernails.

"Never give up hope," August said to him.

He lived on the top floor, right next to the fast-food place. The hamburgers were cold. We sat on the sofa. He yawned, stood up, and disappeared. There was a picture of a young girl hanging over the TV; she looked a little like him. It was very still all of a sudden. Then it started to rain. When I turned around I saw he was undressing and getting into bed. He looked at me and didn't say a word. I don't like to undress in front of men. When I came out of the bathroom, he was asleep.

The rain hammered against the windowpanes, the blinds rattled.

He woke up.

"Oh God," he said. We kissed. He didn't seem so short lying down. His body felt large. He lay on top of me.

"What a beautiful smile you have," he whispered.

We lay there beside one another, saying nothing and holding hands.

"Do you have any brothers or sisters?" he asked.

"Three sisters and one brother. And you?"

"A sister."

"And? Do you get along with her?"

"She's dead."

I never know what to say to that. I'm sorry or some other standard phrase. I said nothing.

"She was murdered. Beaten to death. Her ex-boyfriend beat her to death."

I held his hand more tightly, he pulled it away and sat up in bed.

The rain was getting worse.

"I've got to get those damned blinds fixed. He got three years."

"Only three years?"

"He owns a restaurant where a lot of VIPs go. They all testified on his behalf. He had abused another woman badly once before, but she refused to testify because she was still in love with him."

"I'm sorry." I said.

"My sister had broken up with him. And three months later he showed up, kicked down her garden gate. He dragged her across the yard by the hair. The detectives found a whole bundle of her hair in a plastic bag."

He cried. I watched him. He didn't cry long. The sky turned milky white. The rain let up. He kissed me. Slowly, very slowly he maneuvered himself on top of me. I gave him the biggest smile I knew how to give. He said nothing. When he fell back onto his pillow, he looked ugly. It was day now. He stood up, went to the bathroom, and left the door open. He gagged and vomited into the sink.

"How would you like it if we lived together?" he asked and pulled up the blinds. "I have to throw up every morning. It's awful."

"Maybe it's from smoking too much."

"I don't smoke."

In his underpants he made me a cup of coffee. He is so short, I thought.

I put on my shoes. I spotted a picture of myself on his dresser, a passport photo. My name was written on the back. It was dirty and creased. I'm smiling in the picture. I remember having it made and then not being able to find it again.

I didn't say anything. He opened the door. I could see the gap in his teeth.

A NOTE ON THE TYPE

The text of this book was set in Sabon,
a type face designed by Jan Tschichold
(1902–1974), the well-known German typographer.
Because it was designed in Frankfurt, Sabon was named
for the famous Frankfurt type founder Jacques Sabon,
who died in 1580 while manager
of the Egenolff foundry.
Based loosely on the original designs of
Claude Garamond (c. 1480–1561), Sabon is
unique in that it was explicitly designed
for hot-metal composition on both the
Monotype and Linotype machines
as well as for film composition.

Composed by Crane Typesetting Service, Inc.
West Barnstable, Massachusetts
Printed and bound by Fairfield Graphics
Fairfield, Pennsylvania
Designed by Mia Vander Els